TALES OF ROME

ROME IN FLAMES

Canisbay Sunday Club

D0588982

Presented to

Jeri

By Canisbay Sunday Club
Session 2007/2008

Copyright © Kathy Lee 2005
First published 2005
ISBN 1 84427 089 0

Scripture Union, 207–209 Queensway, Bletchley, Milton Keynes, MK2 2EB, England.
Email: info@scriptureunion.org.uk
Website: www.scriptureunion.org.uk

Scripture Union Australia
Locked Bag 2, Central Coast Business Centre, NSW 2252
Website: www.scriptureunion.org.au

Scripture Union USA
PO Box 987, Valley Forge, PA 19482
Website: www.scriptureunion.org

British Library Cataloguing-in-Publication Data.
A catalogue record of this book is available from the British Library.

Printed and bound in Great Britain by Creative Print and Design (Wales), Ebbw Vale

Internal Illustration by Christopher Rothero
Cover design by GoBallistic
Internal design and layout by Author and Publisher Services

⤷ Scripture Union is an international Christian charity working with churches in more than 130 countries, providing resources to bring the good news about Jesus Christ to children, young people and families and to encourage them to develop spiritually through the Bible and prayer.

As well as our network of volunteers, staff and associates who run holidays, church-based events and school Christian groups, we produce a wide range of publications and support those who use our resources through training programmes.

CONTENTS

Other books by the same author

A Captive in Rome

Fabulous Phoebe
Phoebe's Fortune
Phoebe finds her feet
Phoebe's book of Body Image, Boys and Bible Bits

Seasiders: Runners
Seasiders: Liar
Seasiders: Joker
Seasiders: Winner
Seasiders: Angels

Flood Alert

I

FIRE! FIRE!

How did the fire begin? No one seemed to know. Some people believed it was started deliberately. Others said it was an accident, when a cook dropped a pan of oil, or a child was careless with a candle. It wouldn't be the first time. During the hot summer months, outbreaks of fire were quite common in the city.

But this was no ordinary fire. This was the great fire of Rome.

Like everyone who was there, I can never forget the day it happened – 18 July in the tenth year of the Emperor Nero.

All day a hot, dry wind had been blowing through the streets. It had been unbearable in the baker's shop where I worked, and I was thankful when closing time came.

"What's the matter? Can't take the heat?" Crispus said, grinning. "You ought to be used to it by now."

I'd been working in his shop for two years. Crispus and his wife, Marcella, had been very good to me. They gave me a home and treated me almost like a son, though they had two young children of their own.

Crispus had a round, cheerful face, always ready to smile. Marcella was thinner and more serious-looking. Unlike most Roman women, who loved make-up and jewellery, she dressed very simply. Their home was plain and simple too – a couple of rooms opening off a narrow street in a crowded quarter of the city. It had nothing unusual about it, except the sign of a fish scribbled like a child's drawing beside the door.

The fish was a secret symbol. It stood for the name of Jesus Christ, and showed that Christians, his followers, lived here.

Indoors, Marcella was preparing a meal. "How many are we expecting tonight?" she asked.

Crispus didn't know. Because of the summer heat, many rich people had left the city. Not that many of our Christian friends were rich, but some were slaves to rich men. Tiro, for instance, had gone with his master and his family to their country estate. We probably wouldn't see him for weeks.

Tiro was an African slave who had helped me when I first came to Rome, three years earlier. I'd been captured, along with many others of my tribe, when we tried to rebel against the Romans who had conquered our land. I was sold as a slave. But Tiro bought my freedom, using money that he had been saving up to set himself free. He was the best friend I'd ever had.

If it weren't for Tiro, I would have left Rome long ago, heading for my homeland, Britain. In the city heat, I often felt a stab of homesickness. I longed for summer nights in my own village... cool breezes from the forest... stars as bright as a fox's eyes... and total stillness, unknown in the bustling city.

I didn't know if my village still existed; I couldn't tell if my mother, brother and sisters were still alive. The only way to find out would be to make the long journey home.

If it was God's will, one day I would go back there. One day, when I had repaid Tiro for his gift of my freedom, I would leave Rome behind me for ever.

Someone tapped quietly at the door – three knocks, a pause, and then another knock. It must be one of our friends. Just to make sure, Crispus looked out through the small barred window before unlocking the door. These were dangerous times. As Christians, we couldn't meet openly, because the Emperor Nero hated us. He wanted everyone to worship him as a god, and grew angry when Christians refused to do it. Some of our leaders had already been arrested; a few had been killed.

The only way we could meet together was in secret, in the homes of believers. People arrived quietly after dark. They came in ones and twos, hoping not to be seen.

Then came a louder knock; I went to answer it. The new arrival was Felix. He looked excited, but that wasn't unusual – Felix was always getting excited about something.

Felix had dark hair and mischievous brown eyes. He was 15, a year older than me, although I was a lot taller. (My people, the Celts, are mostly tall and fair-skinned.)

"There's a big fire at the Circus Maximus," he announced. "A really big one! The whole of the Circus is on fire."

The Circus was an enormous place, large enough for chariots to race inside it, with seating all around for thousands of people. I couldn't imagine the entire place being alight. Felix was probably exaggerating.

"Don't you believe me? Come outside and see," he said, grabbing my arm.

By now the sky was almost dark, apart from a red glow above the rooftops to the south. At first I thought it was the remains of the sunset – but the sun doesn't set in the south. That was where the Circus Maximus lay, in the next valley. It must be a bad fire if we could see the light of it from where we were.

"Do you think it will spread?" I asked.

"It will if this wind keeps up," said Felix. "They won't be able to contain it – it's too big."

"I'm glad it isn't blowing this way," I said, feeling sure that we were in no danger. After all, the fire was some distance away, on the far side of the hill. "Come inside, Felix."

Felix was reluctant. He wanted to go back and see the fire – I could tell. Sometimes he acted more like five than 15. He followed me in, though, and started telling everyone about the fire.

"It's God's judgement," said old Cassius, who had a solemn view on everything. "I expect the whole city will perish in flames and destruction."

"Do you think we've come to the end-time?" said Felix eagerly. "The time when Jesus will return?"

"Nobody knows when that will be," said Crispus. "Even our Lord himself didn't know. It might be tomorrow. It might not be for thousands of years."

Felix looked disappointed. Then he brightened up. "If the fire is a judgement from God, maybe we should be out there helping to spread it! We should set fire to the temples of the false gods!"

"No, Felix! It's not up to us to judge other people or punish them," said Cassius. "Only God himself can do that."

One or two people were looking anxious. Titus and Livia, who lived near the Circus Maximus, decided they ought to go home and make sure their belongings were safe. Others followed them. The few of us who remained said prayers for their safety.

After a while we began to hear sounds from the street outside – hurried footsteps, voices shouting, and the cry of a baby. I stared out through the window bars and saw that the narrow street was crowded with people, all heading northwards. Many were loaded down with bundles and bags.

Then I looked up – and caught my breath. That red glow in the sky was much brighter.

Marcella gave a frightened cry. "It's getting closer! What should we do?"

Crispus said, "Get ready to leave if we must. Wake the children up, but don't leave yet. I'll go and find out what's happening."

Felix and I followed him. We had to push through the crowds who were heading the other way –

frightened people, clutching their children and their few possessions. They looked like poor families from the crowded streets by the Circus Maximus.

Near the top of a hill, we found a scene of destruction – but not from the fire. Men were working frantically with hammers, mallets and even their bare hands. They were demolishing buildings, trying to make a gap that the fire could not cross.

We went further, until we could see the fire itself. The valley below us was a bowl of flame. We could hear the roar of it, and smell the charred, bitter smell of burning buildings.

Suddenly my mind leapt back to the day when I was captured. I remembered running through a village that was on fire – Roman soldiers had burned it after the battle where my father had been killed. If I had known then that I would live to see Rome itself blazing like a bonfire, I would have been glad.

But not now. Now I felt anxious for my friends, and sad to see the ruin of so many people's lives. I was frightened, too – I'd never seen a fire like this.

Was there any way to stop it? Would the whole city be destroyed – burned up like a dried leaf in a candle flame?

"Maybe it *is* the end-time." Felix's voice was full of awe. "The end of the world."

II

THE FIREBREAK

"If this keeps up, our home will be in danger," said Crispus. "I must find somewhere safe for Marcella and the children. Maybe we could go to my sister's place..."

I wondered what would happen if Crispus lost his home. The place didn't actually belong to him – it was rented. But if the fire destroyed it, we would be left with no home and no way of earning money.

Crispus noticed my worried look. "It's all right, Bryn," he said quietly. "Whatever happens, our lives are in God's hands."

I knew that – of course I did. But sometimes I forgot to believe it.

Heading back home, we came to the place where men were working to make a firebreak. They were knocking down four-storey buildings, filling the street with rubble. It was a race against time. Would the gap be wide enough to stop the flames from spreading?

"They need more workers," said Felix. "We ought to help them."

He was right. If everyone ran from the fire instead of fighting it, the whole city would soon be in flames. But Crispus looked anxious. I knew he was thinking about Marcella and the children.

"Go home and make sure they're all right," I said. "Felix and I will stay here and help."

"All right, but don't take any risks. This is dangerous work," said Crispus. "May God be with you!"

We looked in the wreckage for some sort of tool to use, and found a couple of heavy metal bars, perhaps from a window.

"These will do," said Felix. "Come on!"

A rickety staircase took us up inside a half-demolished house. At the top, we joined the men who were breaking down the walls. The building was old, with beams rotting and plaster crumbling away.

"This is easy. The place is practically falling apart," said Felix. "Look out below!" He almost seemed to be enjoying himself.

But the fire was creeping closer. Flames licked upwards from doors and windows. As the timber beams burned through, whole buildings came crashing down, and their blazing embers spread the fire in all directions.

Each of the tall buildings, which the Romans called "islands", housed dozens of people. A few had stayed in their homes until the last possible moment, but they were forced to leave when the fire reached their doorsteps. They stumbled towards us through the debris of the firebreak. The flames behind them made their shadows flicker like ghosts.

Some had managed to save a few belongings; others had nothing at all. They looked utterly lost. Where could they go? Who would shelter them?

We had no time to help them. We worked feverishly, hacking away at the building, reducing it to a mound of rubble. By now there were many others helping with the work. A grey-haired man – he looked like a retired soldier – had taken charge of things.

"Right! Move across to the other side of the street," he ordered. "Start at the top of that building there."

But we couldn't get in. The door was barred.

"Go away," came a trembling voice from inside. "This is my home! You can't destroy it!"

"You're a fool," the ex-soldier shouted. "If we don't knock your house down, it's going to burn anyway with you inside it!" He turned to us. "Break the door down!"

Using a wooden beam as a battering ram, we soon knocked down the door. We ran up to the top floor, ignoring the cries of the owner, and started hacking at the roof beams.

By now the fire was actually helping us. Its red, angry glow lit the whole sky, and we could see what we were doing. I noticed that one of the men with us was acting oddly – he seemed to be looking for something hidden in the rafters.

"What are you doing?" Felix demanded, pausing from his work.

"Oh, nothing." The man looked shifty.

One of the other men stopped work too. "I suppose he's looking for the old man's money," he said, in a voice of disgust.

"And why shouldn't I? He's an old miser. He's charged high rents for rooms in this dump for years, and he's never spent any of the money. It must be hidden away somewhere."

Felix stared at him. "Rome is burning, and all you can think about is stealing to make yourself rich? Get out! If you can't help us, get *out*!"

I could see a fight was about to start. But then a section of the roof came crashing in, just missing us. Any hidden treasure was now buried under a heap of broken roof tiles.

Now the flames had reached the far side of the firebreak. I felt the heat of them. I heard the hiss and crackle of burning timber... the sudden *whoosh* as an oil cask exploded... the agonised scream of some trapped creature...

Had we done enough to halt the flames' advance? Was the firebreak wide enough?

"Come down from there!" the ex-soldier shouted. "You don't want to be caught inside if the fire spreads. Come down and help with the water."

Felix and I joined a line of men, which stretched to the nearest fountain. We passed containers from hand to hand – cooking pots, jars, whatever could be found. The men at the front poured water on any sparks that fell on our side of the firebreak. The empty pots came back to be filled again and again.

The air was full of smoke; it stung my throat and made me cough. I was so tired, I felt ready to collapse.

I had no idea how much of the night had gone by. And I couldn't tell how we were doing. Was it possible that the fire beyond our barrier was dying down slightly?

"I think we're winning," Felix said hoarsely, his voice rough with smoke.

If the fire couldn't leap our barrier, it would run out of fuel and burn itself out. Many streets and homes, along with the Circus Maximus, would be reduced to ashes. But the rest of the city would be safe.

My prayers had been answered. Yes – the flames were definitely less fierce. And the eastern sky was lightening with the first pale signs of dawn.

But then I heard a cry of despair. Men were pointing northwards, away from the firebreak.

The street, which had been in darkness, was now lit by flames. Halfway along it, flames were bursting out of a house, leaping into the sky.

"But how?" I gasped. "How could the fire spread so far – and against the wind, too?"

A woman came running down the street. "Help me! Help! They set fire to my house!"

The ex-soldier caught her as she stumbled and almost fell. "What do you mean? Who set fire to your house?"

"I don't know. Men – strangers – they had burning branches and they threw them in."

A murmur of shock ran through the crowd – shock, then anger. We had spent all night fighting the flames. Who had decided to undo all our work?

"Come on," the ex-soldier shouted. "It's not too late. We can still fight it." His voice gave way to a coughing fit.

We were all exhausted, but we might have obeyed him. We might have followed him, like the last weary remnants of an army, and tried to start the battle all over again. But Felix, who had climbed to an upper balcony, called down to us, "It's no use. There are too many fires – five or six at least. We can't fight them all! It's hopeless!"

I ran up the stairs to join him. To the south I could see the main area of the fire – a great ring of flames. To the north and east were smaller, scattered fires. Felix was right. We couldn't possibly fight them all.

"What should we do?" I asked helplessly.

"I'm going home. My mother will be frantic with worry," said Felix, suddenly looking guilty. I knew he was an only child, and his mother was a widow. They lived a few streets away from us.

I said, "Do you think your home will be safe from the fire?"

"Not now. Nor will yours. The safest places will be outside the city – up in the hills, or across the river."

Without wasting any more time, we headed for our homes. Dawn was breaking on a city filled with panic and despair. The streets leading towards the river were crowded with frightened families, trying to reach the bridges that might lead them to safety. I fought my way across the flow of people, and reached home at last.

The door was unlocked, but there was no one inside, only the signs of a hurried exit. My heart sank. Crispus had said something about going to his sister's house, but I had no idea where that was. I'd never met the woman – I wasn't even sure of her name.

Surely they hadn't simply abandoned me? I looked to see if Crispus had left a message of some kind. But there was nothing.

I felt as if I'd been cut off from my own family. Loneliness and fear took a hold of me. What was I to do? Flee from the city? Join that huge crowd of desperate strangers, thousands upon thousands of them, without a friendly face among them? If I did, I might never find Crispus and Marcella again.

Oh God... please help me, show me where I should go... you promised never to leave me...

A sensible thought came into my mind. My friends would expect me to come back here. Crispus might come looking for me once Marcella and the children were safe. I should wait here until he returned.

But what if the fire got here first?

I was too exhausted to care any more. I drank thirstily from the water jar and ate some bread. Then I sank down on my bed.

Mustn't go to sleep. Must watch out for the fire getting closer... oh, but I'm so tired... just rest for a few moments...

I slid down into ocean depths of sleep.

III

Darkness at Noon

I awoke to the sound of voices – quiet, secretive-sounding voices.

I sat up, rubbing my eyes. I don't know who was more surprised – me, or the man who was searching through the chest in the corner of the room. He jumped backwards, and the lid of the chest closed with a bang. His companion, a woman, gave me an uneasy smile.

"Oh, hello, dear," she said. "We thought the place was empty."

Through a fog of sleep, I realised that I knew these people. They lived at the end of the street and sold cloth in the market.

"What do you think you're doing?" I said angrily, rubbing my eyes again. My clouded vision did not clear, and I suddenly realised why. This mistiness was smoke! The fire!

I jumped out of bed and ran to the window. There were no flames outside – not yet. A grey fog of drifting smoke filled the air, and the sky was as dark as a thundercloud.

"Don't worry, love," said the woman, Julia. "It hasn't reached the end of the street yet. We just thought we'd try to save what we could before it gets here. Didn't we, Flavius?"

"*Save?* Don't you mean *steal?*" I said.

"Oh, you can't call it stealing," Flavius objected. "Not when the owners have abandoned everything. We saw them go, carrying as much as they could. And I said to myself, there's bound to be more in there for the taking."

"How do you know they won't be coming back?" I demanded.

"What – risk their lives for the sake of a few belongings and a slave? Not likely, is it? Look, why don't you help yourself? There's more here than we can carry. And if we don't take it, it will all go up in flames, so where's the harm?"

"I am not a slave," I said, coldly. "Crispus is my friend, not my master. And he'll be coming back. So you'd better not be here when he does! Get out!"

"All right, all right. No harm done," said Flavius. "We'll try next door."

"We didn't realise Crispus owned such a faithful guard dog," said Julia spitefully.

They went out, and the door banged behind them.

I still felt angry. How could people be so greedy and selfish? I began to wonder about those outbreaks of fire, which had started as the main fire was dying down. Perhaps they had been lit by thieves and looters, willing to destroy whole streets so that they could steal what they wanted.

But at least Flavius and Julia had reminded me of something. I mustn't forget to take my most precious possession – the writing that proved I was a freedman, not a slave. After Tiro gave me my freedom, he had the official documents made out for me, so that there could be no question about the matter. I put the little scroll in my money pouch and hung it round my neck.

I went to the door, hoping to see Crispus approaching. But the smoke was so thick, I could hardly see across the street. I began coughing and couldn't stop.

Crowds of people were still on the move. I saw a lost child, separated from her parents, crying bitterly. Old people gasped for breath, choking in the smoke. A rich man was carried past on a couch held by slaves. But all his money couldn't buy him safety from the fire – he looked as scared as everyone else.

How long should I wait? I would have to make a move before long. I decided I'd go when the fire reached the end of our street. And that would be soon; I could see a red glow to the south.

I had no idea where to go. To the hills or across the river, Felix had said. But what would I do when I got there? I had hardly any money. I didn't know anyone outside the city.

Whatever happened, I had to get moving. I searched for anything that might be useful. I bundled things up in my spare cloak - a knife, a cooking pot, some cheese, a loaf of bread - whatever I could find. It took my mind off the loneliness and the fear.

Crispus wouldn't come back. I knew that now. He didn't really care about me. He wouldn't risk his life to come back looking for me.

Miserably, I gathered my things together and headed for the door, giving one last look back. I had been happy here; I thought I'd found a family to belong to. But I'd been fooling myself. This was not my home. Why should I care if it went up in flames?

I stepped out into the moving crowd and let it sweep me along. The smoke was even thicker now. I took shallow, gasping breaths, trying not to cough. The hour must be around midday, although it was dark enough to be evening.

"Bryn! Over here!"

It sounded like Crispus, but I couldn't see him. Then the crowd parted for a second. Crispus struggled towards me like a half-drowned man fighting his way through a flooded river.

"Thank God I found you," he gasped. "Don't go westward. The whole city is trying to cross the bridges - it's madness."

"Where should we go, then?"

"To my sister Domitia's house. Marcella and the children are there already. It's on the northern edge of Rome. If the fire gets that far, at least we can escape into open country. Here, take my arm - we don't want to get separated."

I was sorry that I'd doubted him. Suddenly my heart felt light. There was still danger... but at least I didn't have to face it alone.

Getting across the city took ages. As we went further north, the crowds hardly seemed to lessen, but they were moving more freely and all heading in the same direction. Crispus and I stopped to help a woman who was trying to cope with three small children. I picked up one of them, ignoring his protests.

"Put me down! I want to go home!" he howled, struggling in my arms. How could I explain that his home might not exist any more?

Crispus asked the woman where she was going.

"I don't know," she said, helplessly. "And one of these boys isn't even mine. I was looking after him for a neighbour. How am I ever going to find her again?"

We helped her as far as a temple on the Via Flaminia, where her husband had told her to wait for him. "He sent us on ahead. His father's got the marsh fever so badly he can hardly walk. They're back there somewhere..."

"Would you like us to wait with you?" I asked her.

"No – you go on. They might take hours to get here."

Or they might never arrive. But what could we do? We left her sitting on the temple steps, clutching the children close to her, and gazing into the crowd that swirled past. I have no idea what happened to her.

On the crest of the Quirinal Hill, where the air was less smoky, we looked back over Rome. All across the city lay a huge, dark cloud, lit here and there by glowing tongues of flame. Thousands of homes must have vanished for ever, along with shops, temples, markets, bathhouses... Our own home was probably ablaze by now. Like countless other people, we were homeless.

But at least Crispus and I had somewhere to go. "It's not far now to my sister's place," he said. "Just down the hill."

"Is your sister rich, then?" I said, surprised. We were in an area where all the houses were large and luxurious. My old master's house wasn't far away.

"Domitia married a rich man," said Crispus. "My father thought he'd found a good husband for her, even though Septimus was just a freed slave, not a citizen. He was making himself rich, and my parents thought that was all that mattered."

"How did he make his money?" I asked.

"By shipping slaves in from the East and selling them at a vast profit. Now he owns a big house and a country estate. He's trying to make people forget that he was once a slave himself. So we don't see much of Domitia these days. We're not grand enough for Septimus."

"What did they say when you suddenly arrived?" I asked.

"Well, Domitia is my sister. She welcomed us in and said we can stay as long as we need to. But I could tell Septimus wasn't exactly overjoyed."

"You sound as if you don't get on too well with him."

"No. You'll see why when you meet him. I think you'll like Domitia, though."

I did like her. She came hurrying to meet us as soon as the slaves announced our arrival. She was small and very pretty, with dark curly hair and a quick smile. She wore masses of expensive jewellery, which reminded me of my old master's wife. But she wasn't the least bit snobbish or proud.

"Oh, Crispus, I'm so glad you've got back safely. I was worried about you! And this must be Bryn." She smiled at me. "Crispus has told me all about you. You are welcome here – come in."

And in we went.

IV

SEPTIMUS

The last time I was in a house as grand as this, I was a kitchen slave. Now I was a guest of the family, lying on a couch while respectful slaves served up a rich meal – oysters, fish pasties, boars' ribs, roast duck. There was more meat on the table than we normally ate in a month. Maybe Septimus was trying to impress his wife's poor relations. Or maybe he always ate like this, fire or no fire.

Septimus looked 20 years older than Domitia; she could have been his daughter, not his wife. He was plump and bald, with a broad, beaming smile. His eyes, though, were very sharp. His face smiled, but his eyes didn't join in.

Of course the main talking point was the fire. Crispus and I described what we had seen – the chaos in the streets, the failed attempts to contain the fire – and Domitia grew pale.

"Do you really think it will reach as far as here?" she asked her brother.

"Of course it won't," Septimus interrupted. "Our divine, all-powerful Emperor would never permit that."

Was he serious? How could the Emperor – even though he was supposed to be a god – do anything to save the city?

As a Christian, I didn't believe the Emperor had divine powers. Nero was only a man – an evil man, some people said, or a vain fool who believed he was a genius. He did have enormous power, of course. Being Emperor, he could have his enemies imprisoned or even killed. So it was safer not to say anything against him.

Septimus said, "I heard today from a friend of mine – a senator, no less – that our Emperor was seen last night in the streets, helping to fight the flames. Then, when he grew tired of heroic deeds, he retreated to his palace and sang songs about the fall of Troy."

His voice was sarcastic, and I saw he didn't believe the Emperor was godlike any more than I did. However, I guessed he was being careful not to say anything that would make him sound openly rebellious. Even at home, it wasn't safe to speak freely. A man's own slaves might betray him.

"The Emperor had better look out," said Crispus. "His palace lies right in the path of the fire. I wouldn't be surprised if it was ablaze by now."

Marcella shot him a warning look. What he had said could easily be twisted to sound as if he *wanted* the palace to catch fire.

Domitia said to her husband, "Perhaps we should be preparing to remove our most valuable things. Should I tell the slaves—"

Again Septimus interrupted her – quite rudely, I thought. "I've taken care of that. Two carriageloads went off to our country place this afternoon. Even if the fire doesn't reach us here, there may be a danger of theft and looting."

"There already is," I said, and I told Crispus and Marcella about their thieving neighbours. They seemed taken aback.

"Not that they would have found much worth stealing," said Crispus, and Septimus gave him a scornful glance. He obviously thought that Crispus, a humble baker, couldn't own *anything* worth stealing. "It's just that... well, they were our neighbours."

"I'm afraid this is what we have to expect," said Septimus. "Breakdown of law and order, everyone out for what they can get... We should arm ourselves. We should be prepared."

Marcella looked worried, and I guessed she was thinking of the children. They were already in bed, in the care of the slaves who looked after Domitia's young daughter, Ursula.

Although Marcella had been very quiet during the meal, she ventured to speak now. "Don't you think we would be safer at your place in the country?" she asked Domitia.

Once again, Septimus cut in, as though his wife's opinion was quite unimportant. "There's no need to panic just yet, my dear Marcella. If the fire comes close, we shall have plenty of warning."

"But think of Ursula and the other children," Domitia said. "They would be so much better off—"

"Silence, woman!" her husband snapped. "Don't argue! Who is the master of this house?"

"You are, my lord." Domitia bowed her head.

He glared at her. Then, with an effort, he controlled his anger. "In any case, you can't leave until the carriages return from the villa. Not unless you're willing to walk there. It's a good 15 miles."

"The little ones can't possibly walk that far," said Crispus. "We must wait until the carriages come back."

Marcella was silent. But I could guess what she was thinking. Septimus cared more for his precious possessions than for his family! He had sent two carriageloads of valuables to safety, while keeping his wife and child here in the danger area.

I didn't much like Septimus, who had ignored me during the entire meal. I liked him even less when he suddenly started talking to me. He asked about my homeland – what the people were like, and how long the journey took from Britain to Rome.

"Why? Are you planning to visit Britain?" I asked him.

"Oh, no. But I might think of doing some trade in that direction. I could send my men to buy slaves there. British slaves fetch an excellent price at the moment."

"I can't think why," I said. "If they are like I was when I first came to Rome, they'll make useless slaves – stubborn, hard to train, and totally ignorant of your language." Of course I didn't want Septimus, or anyone like him, buying and selling my own people.

Septimus laughed. "Oh, it's all a matter of fashion. A few years ago everyone wanted Nubian slaves, but now they must have Britons. I simply supply what people demand. And I've done rather well out of it, as you can see." He waved his arm around the dining room, with its beautiful painted walls and mosaic floor, which must have cost the price of 50 slaves.

Horrible man! But we were guests in his house. We must be polite and grateful to him for taking us in, although I could see that Marcella didn't like him either. She was never very good at hiding her feelings.

It was a relief when the meal was over and we went to our bedrooms. Mine was on an upper floor, with a window looking out on an enclosed garden. I wished I could look out in the other direction, to see if the fire was coming closer.

The room was very grand. There were silver statues here and there, and empty niches where other ornaments had been hurriedly removed. The bed was the biggest and most luxurious that I had ever seen. But I wasn't at all sure I would be able to sleep.

Crispus tapped quietly on my door. "Marcella and I are going to pray together. Would you like to join us?"

When we prayed, I began to feel calmer. I remembered that my life was in God's hands, wherever I was – in a burning slum or a rich man's house, in the city or the country, anywhere. So there was nothing to fear, not even death itself.

As a Christian, I believed that death was the gateway to heaven. All the same, I didn't want to die...

not just yet. I prayed that the fire would somehow be halted, that the rest of the city would be saved, and that no more people would be killed.

We prayed for everyone we knew. Felix and his mother; Titus; Livia; and all the other believers... We had no idea where they were, or even if they were still alive.

"And now," said Crispus, "it's time for bed. Get as much sleep as you can. Only God knows what tomorrow will bring."

V

GO BACK!

Next day, it seemed that the sun did not rise. The air grew a little lighter, that was all. A dark, smoky cloud hung over the city – the fire was still burning.

But the slaves sent out by Septimus came back with good news. A large area had been cleared to make a gigantic firebreak, which lay between us and the flames. Hopefully, the northern side of the city would be safe.

"I told you there was no need to panic," said Septimus. He turned to Domitia. "Next time, pay attention to what I say."

"Next time? I hope there isn't going to be a next time," said Crispus. "This is Rome's worst disaster in centuries."

Septimus said coldly, "I meant, next time my wife thinks she knows better than I do. A bad habit, don't you agree? A wife should never argue with her lord and master."

Domitia flinched at the harsh tone of his voice, and I wondered if Septimus was cruel to her. He seemed to expect her to obey him like a slave – and I was pretty sure his slaves weren't treated too well. They were unnaturally silent and watchful as they went about their duties. People often say that an ex-slave is a bad master.

Later, I asked Crispus about Domitia. We were out in the garden, keeping an eye on the children. They played quietly by the fountain. They were overawed by this strange, new place, and the brooding darkness of the sky. Every now and then, they would glance over to where we were sitting, as if to make sure their parents were still there. Then they would return to their game.

"This is a beautiful house," I said. "But is your sister happy here?"

Crispus looked all around, making sure no one could overhear us. "No," he said. "I don't think she is."

"Your parents should never have married her to that man," said Marcella. "Anyone can see he doesn't love her or care for her." She glanced up at her husband, as if to say, "Not like you care for me."

"She hasn't been able to give him a son. That's part of the problem," said Crispus.

"They have a daughter, though, don't they?" I said.

"Septimus isn't interested in daughters. He says they're a waste of time and money. After Ursula, Domitia had two more daughters, but Septimus refused to keep them." His face was grim.

Of course, I knew about the Roman way of dealing with unwanted babies. They were simply abandoned – left outside to die.

"He told her to forget they had ever been born," said Marcella. "But she still grieves for them. Can you blame her?"

***

As the day wore on, I began to feel restless. It was strange to have no work to do. I decided that the life of a rich Roman wasn't for me. I simply couldn't sit around all day, with slaves to fetch and carry for me – the boredom would kill me.

In the afternoon, when the restless feeling grew too much, I decided to go out and see if the fire was still spreading.

"Do be careful, Bryn," said Crispus. "Make sure you're back here by nightfall."

In the street outside, things looked almost normal. There were still a few people heading towards the outskirts of the city, but nearly as many were coming back in. Perhaps they were curious, like me. Perhaps they were looking for their families or friends.

But the weather was far from normal-looking. The sky was threateningly black, as if a heavy snowstorm was about to begin. No snow fell, but white flakes of ash came drifting down. The air felt hot, dry, and gritty. I was so used to the smell of smoke that I almost didn't notice it any more. I went to the top of a hill, hoping to see what was happening to the south. But I was looking through a thick fog, which blurred the edges of everything. I couldn't even guess how far the fire had progressed.

I knew this area quite well from my time as a slave. My old master's house must be just around the corner. Suddenly I felt curious to see the place again.

The big front doors were closed. I remembered that the family had gone to their country villa before the hot weather came, and my friend Tiro, the coachman, had gone with them. Probably there were just a few slaves left in charge of the house.

I didn't bother to knock at the door. As a disgraced ex-slave, sold for stealing the master's property, I would hardly be welcome here. From the outside, the house looked the same as ever. I walked around the side, towards the doors that led to the stables. They would be locked, the stables empty. But that was odd – I could definitely hear the whinny of a horse.

Then the big doors swung open. I heard the sound of hooves, and out came the coach and its four black horses, with Tiro in the driving seat. When he saw me, he reined in the horses.

"Bryn! Good to see you! But why are you here?"

I told him how we had lost our home. "We got out all right. I don't know about any of our friends, though. Have you heard from anyone?"

Tiro shook his head. "I only got here this morning, and now I'm going back to the villa. We heard about the fire – in fact we could see the smoke of it from ten miles away. The master sent us to fetch his strongbox with all his money and documents."

I looked into the carriage. The strongbox, a heavy, metal-bound chest, was guarded by two tough-looking slaves. I didn't recognise either of them – perhaps they were from the master's farm.

"Can I ride with you for a little way?" I asked.

Tiro hesitated, then said, "All right. You mustn't come far, though. I don't want you getting into danger. The main road eastwards was clear this morning, but the fire's still burning..."

I climbed up onto the seat beside him. "Don't worry," he called over his shoulder to the two guards. "This is Bryn – he's an old friend of mine."

Tiro flicked the reins, and the horses set off. They were quite nervous of the smoke and the strange smells, but Tiro handled them expertly.

We were heading south-eastwards, and the smoke grew thicker. Soon we came to the edge of the firebreak Septimus' slaves had described. Dozens of buildings had been reduced to rubble. The coach couldn't cross this area; we had to go around it, through narrow streets, which hadn't been designed for coaches.

These streets were crowded. People were on the move, looking lost and frightened. Their homes had been burned or destroyed, all their possessions were gone, and now they didn't know where to go. Some of them gave us angry looks. Why were we riding in a carriage, guarding a rich man's property, when they had to walk?

A man called out, "It's all right for the rich. You don't see rich men's houses being knocked down, do you? Oh no. It's always the poor who get trodden on!"

People jostled the sides of the carriage. The two big slaves gripped their weapons and got ready to fight if they had to.

"I shouldn't have let you come with us," Tiro said to me. He looked anxious. "You don't want to get mixed up in this. Get down – go back."

I started to argue, because I didn't want to climb down into that hostile crowd. I felt safer up on the carriage seat next to Tiro.

But ahead of us something was happening. The crowd was backing up in the narrow street. Over their heads I could see a line of soldiers, barring the way. They belonged to the Emperor's Praetorian Guard – the only troops allowed in the city.

"You can't get through here," their leader shouted. "The fire is too close. Go back!"

People began to surge past us, going back the way we had come. But there was no room for us to turn round in that narrow space. And it was impossible for the horses to push the carriage backwards up the hill.

Tiro shouted to the captain of the guard. "What am I supposed to do? I can't go back."

"Get down and walk, then. Just get out of here!"

"No. I'm not leaving the horses."

The captain shrugged. "Very well then, it's up to you. Try to get through if you want to. But don't blame me if you don't make it!"

He motioned to his men to stand aside. The street ahead was empty – empty of people, that is. It was full of swirling smoke. But I couldn't see any signs of flames. Perhaps the soldiers were being too cautious.

Tiro got the horses moving. Suddenly, as we turned a corner, two men ran across the road in front of us. They carried flaming branches, which made the horses shy away. Almost before we had time to see them, the men disappeared into a building.

Was I mistaken, or were they soldiers? What were they doing?

But there was no time to think about that. Ahead of us, through the smoke, I could see a flickering red glow. Fire!

The horses saw it too. They came to a stop, snorting and trampling the ground. They refused to go forward, even when Tiro used his whip.

"I'll have to unhitch the horses and lead them back the way we came," said Tiro grimly.

"What about the carriage?" demanded one of the slaves. "And the master's strongbox?"

"You can carry the strongbox between you, can't you?" said Tiro. "As for the carriage, let it burn. Come on! Let's get moving!"

"But Tiro! Look!" I gasped, pointing back up the hill.

Flames were leaping out from the windows of a building. There was fire behind us as well as in front – we were trapped.

VI

THROUGH THE FLAMES

Tiro shouted to one of the slaves in the carriage. "Aulus! Take the reins for me. I'm going to see how bad it is up ahead. Quickly now!"

Aulus climbed up onto the driver's seat, and Tiro jumped down, running into the swirling smoke. Aulus held the reins nervously. He looked as if he was more used to controlling oxen than horses.

Very soon Tiro returned. The smoke was making him cough so badly that he could hardly speak. "There's a chance we can get through. The road widens out - marketplace or something. Fire's only on one side. The horses may get past it if I guide them."

He stood by the leading pair of horses, talking to them, calming them. "Easy now, Victor. It's all right. Easy, Tuscus."

It was amazing how they responded to his voice. They even walked forwards for a few paces. But then, as the glow of the fire grew brighter, fear gripped them again. Victor tried to rear up. For an instant I thought Tiro would be trampled under his hooves.

"Tiro!" I cried in terror.

But he was still there. He managed to hold the horses. "Bryn!" he called up to me. "Is there a cloak under my seat? Bring it here."

Tiro wrapped the cloak around Victor's head, covering his eyes. When the horse couldn't see the flames, he calmed down a little, and Tiro talked to him steadily, soothingly.

"Now then, there's nothing to fear. On we go." He carried on talking, so that the horse could still hear him. Amazingly, Victor seemed to trust him completely. He walked forwards as if Tiro was guiding him into his own stable. The others, although still nervous, took their lead from him.

Tiro took them as far to the left as possible, for the fire was on the right. It loomed closer, and I could feel the heat of it - and the pain when a burning spark caught me on the face.

Oh, God... please get us safely through this...

Still the horses went forwards. Only one building seemed to be ablaze. Beyond it lay safety.

We were alongside it - we were past it - we were through!

I couldn't believe it. Nor could the soldiers who were guarding the far end of the street. When we came at them out of the smoke, they looked at us as if they thought we were ghosts.

"By all the gods! How did they get a coach and horses through *that?*" I heard one of them say.

"Tiro, that was amazing," I told him, as he climbed up to take the reins again.

"Oh well, the horses know me," he said. "I've looked after them for years. Now where are we?"

He asked the soldiers how to reach the main road leading eastwards from the city. They gave him directions, warning him to avoid the Emperor's palace, for it was ablaze.

The Emperor's palace! If this was true, then the whole centre of Rome must have gone up in flames. And the fire was still spreading!

"I ought to go back," I said. "Crispus and Marcella will be wondering where I am."

Tiro looked anxious. "Don't try to go back across the city. Keep to the outskirts. God go with you!"

***

It took me a long time to find my way back to Septimus' house. I went around the north-eastern fringes of the city. In the fields beyond, dozens of homeless people were trying to make shelters for the night. They looked hungry, exhausted and scared.

I told myself to be thankful that I had a house to go to. If only it was a different house! I didn't like Septimus' place, full of useless luxuries. I didn't like the silent, well-trained slaves who seemed to sneer when they looked at me. And I didn't like Septimus himself.

He apologised for the evening meal. The cook had done his best with the things in his store cupboard, for of course it was impossible to buy fresh food at the moment... But the meal was still lavish, and I thought of those homeless people who might have eaten nothing for two days.

I told them what had happened that afternoon. "The fire's still spreading. The Emperor's palace has gone up in flames."

"The palace?" Marcella looked dismayed.

"Don't worry," said Crispus. "The Emperor can easily afford to rebuild it. He won't be homeless for very long."

"It's not the Emperor I'm worried about," said Marcella. "It's the whole of Rome. What else has been destroyed?"

"Many great buildings, I hear," said Septimus. "The temple of Jupiter, the Atrium Vestae - all gone."

Everyone was silent. It was hard to believe what was happening... the destruction of the greatest city ever known. Perhaps Felix had been right when he said we were facing the last days, the end of the world.

"But don't look so miserable!" said Septimus. "You're quite right, Crispus. Everything will be rebuilt. Rome may become even better than before. And think how much money will be spent in doing it. There will be a huge demand for skilled slaves - masons and carpenters and artists. I must get hold of a good selection before the price goes up."

While he was talking, a slave had come into the room with a message for Domitia. Her daughter Ursula was ill. Domitia got up and slipped out of the room, without a word to her husband.

She still had not come back by the time we finished eating. Marcella went to find out if the little girl was all right.

When Marcella returned, she looked worried. "Ursula is having trouble breathing," she said. "Perhaps it's all the smoke in the air. Her breath sounds like the wheezing of an old woman."

Septimus didn't seem particularly bothered. "Oh, this happens all the time," he said. "She's a sickly child – always has something wrong with her. Domitia spoils her, that's the trouble."

"But this looks serious," said Marcella. "You should send for a doctor."

"It wouldn't do any good. The doctors all say different things about this breathing sickness. Garlic... pepper... cinnamon... Their advice is worthless. All it does is make them rich at my expense."

Marcella looked as if she wanted to shout at him. She kept calm, but I could tell that it took an effort. "Maybe, then, we should get Ursula out of the city. She might breathe more easily in cleaner air."

"Yes, yes. If the carriage is back, I suppose she can go tomorrow."

***

Crispus woke me in the middle of the night. His voice was low and urgent.

"We're going to pray for Ursula. She's very sick – perhaps dying. Will you come?"

The little girl was lying on her bed. In the lamplight, her skin looked pale, almost blue-white. Although her eyes were open, she didn't seem to see anything. Her only movement was her struggle for breath.

Domitia was holding her hand. Silent tears rolled down her cheeks, the tears of a mother who can do nothing to help her child. Two slaves stood by, looking equally helpless. There was no sign of Septimus.

Crispus sent a slave to fetch some oil. He dipped his hand in it, stroked it on Ursula's forehead, and started to pray.

For a long time we prayed, but nothing seemed to happen. Then – or was I imagining things? – I sensed a change in Ursula. Her rasping, wheezy breath was a little quieter. Her face wasn't quite so deathly pale.

"God be praised," whispered Marcella.

Slowly the light of dawn crept into the room. Slowly Ursula's breathing grew easier, until it was almost normal. Her eyelids drooped, and she slid into an exhausted sleep.

Domitia hugged her brother. "How can I ever thank you?" she said.

"It isn't us you should be thanking," he said gently.

"The god that you prayed to – I must make him an offering. What would be suitable? A lamb? A white calf?"

"God doesn't want our offerings... Only our love."

Domitia looked bewildered. "I don't understand. A god who doesn't want offerings?"

"Don't worry." Crispus gave a huge yawn. "Get some sleep, Domitia. We'll talk about it later."

VII

THE ROAD FROM ROME

The fire had now been burning for three nights and two days with no sign of dying down. And Rome was falling apart.

Even in the area that the fire had not touched, it was impossible to carry on living a normal life. No food supplies were coming into the city. No shops were open. It seemed as if people were afraid to stay in their homes and afraid to leave them.

Domitia was desperate to get Ursula out of the city, away from the smoke, which was so bad for her breathing. It would be safer at the country villa, and there would be no problems finding food.

But Septimus was equally determined to stay. "I'm not leaving this house to be burgled and looted," he said.

Domitia said, "The household slaves will still be here. They could take care of the place."

"You can't trust slaves if they're left on their own," said Septimus, darkly. "They would steal from their own mothers. They have no loyalty to anyone but themselves."

And whose fault is that? I felt like asking him. Few slaves would be loyal to a harsh master. I thought of Tiro, risking danger by coming into the city on the master's orders. But then Lucius, his master, was a decent man who had always treated his slaves fairly well.

In the end it was decided that Septimus would stay in Rome. The rest of us would go to the villa. It was 15 miles away, a journey that should only take a few hours by carriage.

But the road was crowded with people, a slow-moving mass of refugees. Some were exhausted; some were supporting old people or small children. Some, it seemed, went slowly because they didn't know where they were going. Their faces blank and hopeless, they simply let the crowd tow them along.

By midday we had covered only a few miles. We came to a small town, which looked as if it would usually be a quiet, sleepy place. Now it was crowded with the homeless people of Rome. They had set up camp under the arches of the forum and on the steps of a temple. They were queuing to buy food at three times the normal price – those who had money, that is.

What would happen to them? A few days ago, they had been at home or at work, living safe, ordinary, boring lives. Suddenly everything had been turned upside down and shaken out like corn from a sack. Nothing would ever be the same again.

I looked back towards the city. It was invisible under its cloud of dark smoke. All around us was bright sunlight and the singing of birds, and yet the smell of smoke still lingered. People had brought it with them. Their clothes were black with it.

Domitia looked at the crowds with pity and dismay. "I wish we could help them. But Septimus warned me not to take in any more refugees."

This didn't surprise me. Septimus only cared about himself and his own comfort. He could live quite happily in his enormous house, while homeless people streamed past the door.

"Are we nearly there yet?" Ursula asked for the twentieth time. She was bored with riding in the carriage – unlike Marcella's children in the carriage behind. They had never done this before (in fact, they had hardly ever been outside the city), and they were entranced.

Domitia told her the journey was half over. We had left the small town behind us, and the road was quieter. Only a few stragglers were walking along it, or sitting down by the roadside when they could walk no further. It was hot, and the road was dusty and dry.

The coachman asked permission to give the horses a rest; we halted in the shade of some trees. Not far away, I saw that a woman had collapsed on the ground. A young man was trying to help her to her feet.

"Come on, Mother. We must go on a bit further – just a little bit. It's not far to the next village... We'll get water there..."

The voice sounded familiar. I looked again.

"Felix!" I cried.

He turned and stared, taking in the strange sight of his friends riding in carriages, like rich people. Felix himself, with his sooty clothes and smoke-blackened face, looked just the opposite – the poorest of the poor. Normally full of energy, he seemed exhausted. His mother looked even worse. Her face was as grey and worn as an old bit of rag.

Crispus and I got out and ran to him. "Are you all right, Felix?"

"Not too bad. But my mother's ill. I don't think she can walk any further. We've had no food since yesterday morning."

"Where are you heading for?" I asked him, thinking that perhaps we could take him part of the way.

He shrugged helplessly. "Anywhere. I thought that maybe I could find work on a farm in return for food. We don't have any money."

Marcella brought some bread and a jar of water.

"Oh, you're an answer to my prayers!" said Felix. He ate hungrily, but his mother had got past the stage of wanting food. She swallowed a few gulps of water, then sank down again.

I looked at Crispus. "Couldn't we take them to the villa with us?"

"That's up to Domitia. It's her house, or rather Septimus'. And you know what Septimus said about no more refugees."

He went over to his sister and they talked in low voices. I could see that Domitia was being torn two ways. She wanted to help her brother's friend, but also she was afraid. Every now and then she glanced at the coachman, as if he might be spying on her for Septimus.

I went closer. Crispus was reminding Domitia about last night. "You wanted to make an offering to God. You wanted to thank him for answering our prayers. Well, our God doesn't want animal sacrifices, but he is glad when we obey him, when we love other people and help them..."

Still Domitia looked afraid. I saw Felix's hopeful face, and his mother's hopeless one. Then I had a thought.

"Septimus said no more refugees in his house at Rome," I said. "He didn't even mention the villa, I bet."

She hesitated for a moment. Then a smile brightened her face. "You're absolutely right! So I won't be disobeying him, will I?"

My heart filled with relief. Domitia said, "Tell your friends they may come with us if they want to."

We rearranged all the passengers, and helped Felix to lift his mother into a carriage. It was rather a squash now, but no one minded.

Crispus' son looked at Felix's smoke-smudged face. "Were you in the big fire? Did you get burned?"

"Very nearly," said Felix, and he told the story of his escape from Rome. He made it sound as adventurous as possible. "We were trying to get across one of the bridges. But it was narrow, like the neck of a bottle, and so crowded that we couldn't get near it. People were pushing and shoving... We almost got crushed to death."

The children stared at him, round-eyed. "So how did you get out?"

"We gave up trying to cross the river. Instead, we found our way across the city and got out on the northern side, furthest away from the fire. That's when I realised all my money was missing. Maybe I dropped it in the crush; maybe someone stole it. Oh, that was a bad moment... But I prayed to God, and I knew that somehow he would help us."

I asked if Felix had news of any of our other friends.

"I did see Titus," he said. "He got separated from Livia in the crowd and couldn't find her again. He was going back into the city to look for her. But he didn't even know if she was still alive."

I told him about my journey with Tiro the previous day. When I mentioned the sudden new outbreaks of fire, Felix nodded. "That's been happening all over the place. Some people are saying the fire was started deliberately." Then he lowered his voice so that the coachman would not hear us. "And they say it was done on the Emperor's orders."

"But that's crazy," I said. "The Emperor's own palace was destroyed in the fire. Why would he want that to happen?"

"Ah, well... He might have his reasons."

"What reasons?" Crispus demanded.

"This is what people are saying – it's only a rumour, of course. They say Nero has always wanted to build himself an enormous new palace right in the centre of Rome. The fire will give him the excuse to do it, and free up the land he needs."

Unbelievable! Yet I couldn't help wondering...

It had been soldiers – the Emperor's men – who had blocked off that street just before the fire broke out. And although I couldn't swear to it, I believed that the men with lit branches were soldiers, too.

"Nero is an evil man," said Crispus quietly. "He'll stop at nothing to get what he wants."

"They say that too much power can make men mad," said Felix. "The question is, what will the madman want next?"

VIII

IN THE COUNTRY

The country villa was a large old house set among cornfields and olive groves. It was a quiet, sleepy place, much more pleasant than the big house in Rome. Marcella's children loved it. And shy little Ursula began to come out of her shell. She showed the others around the farm, letting them feed the doves and watch the goats being milked.

I liked the place too. I had some bad memories of Roman farms. But this place was nothing like the vineyard where I had spent one dreadful summer as a slave. Here the farm manager treated his slaves fairly. He didn't believe in using chain gangs or harsh punishments. So his men stayed healthy and worked well without too much trouble.

Felix's mother soon looked almost well again. Felix was extremely grateful to Domitia.

"When you brought us here, you saved my mother's life," Felix told her. "I wish I could repay you somehow.

I haven't got any money, but I could work on the farm."

Domitia laughed. "Don't be silly. You are my guests for as long as you want to stay."

We all knew that we couldn't stay forever, living on Domitia's kindness. Crispus and I would have to look for work. Perhaps we would return to Rome – although not yet. It was almost a week since the fire broke out, but we could still see that ominous plume of smoke on the horizon.

Maybe we could set up shop in some other town. "We must pray for God to guide us," said Crispus.

Felix said, "It's all right for you. A baker can easily find work – people will always need bread. But what about me?"

Felix had been halfway through his apprenticeship to a silversmith. But the workshop had gone up in flames, and Felix had no idea what had happened to his employer. Besides, in times of crisis, silversmiths were not exactly in demand.

"I'd be better off if I'd learned carpentry or something," he said, gloomily. "Those skills will be needed when Rome is rebuilt."

"If it ever is rebuilt," said Domitia. "If there's anything left of it."

She sounded as if she hardly cared one way or the other. I thought she would be quite content to live here forever.

But I was starting to feel hungry for news of the city. What was happening there? What would become of all the homeless people who were scattered around, living rough? Some of our friends might be among them...

One day, Felix and I walked to the nearest village to find out if there was any news. At the fountain, we met a farmer and his son with an empty ox cart. The oxen looked dusty and tired, as if they had travelled a long way. And my guess was right – they had come from Rome.

"We took a load of vegetables to sell," the man said. "We heard you could get good prices, and it was true. There's not enough food getting into the city, or to the outskirts where people are camping out. We sold the lot before we had even reached the gates. Look – a woman gave me this for a bag of beans."

He showed us a gold ring. I guessed it was worth much more than a bag of beans... but not to someone who was hungry. You can't eat gold.

"It was a profitable trip, then?" I said.

The farmer nodded, but he didn't seem particularly happy. Nor did his son. They both looked a bit shocked.

"You should see what's happened to Rome," the boy said. "It's ruined!"

"Yes. I've never seen anything like it," his father said, grimly.

"Is the fire still burning?" Felix asked.

"Not any more. But it's taken the heart out of Rome. Whole districts have been laid flat. My cousin lives near the Theatre of Marcellus – used to, that is. I couldn't find his apartment or his street, or even the Theatre. All that's left is a pile of rubble."

I tried to tell him that his cousin might still be alive. "Lots of people managed to escape from the fire. They fled into the countryside, or to nearby towns."

The farmer shook his head. "He would have come to us if he'd been left homeless. I think he must have died in the fire..."

The oxen had finished drinking. Wearily, the man got back in the cart. "Come on," he said to his son. "I want to get home before nightfall."

We went back to the villa, feeling depressed. There had been many things wrong with Rome, such as the stinking slums of the Suburra, and the splendid, wasteful homes on the Palatine Hill. All the same, it had been an impressive city. I could still remember the awe I'd felt when I first arrived. Those great, pillared temples, the spacious forum, the busy markets... That mixture of people from all the corners of the earth...

Maybe Septimus was right. The city would be rebuilt, perhaps even better than before. But that would take years, and in the meantime, people still had to live. What would happen to all those homeless families when winter arrived?

When we got back, the others were sitting in the garden. The villa had a beautiful garden, laid out in terraces on the hillside, with ilex trees to give shade from the sun. Crispus and Domitia were deep in conversation.

Domitia said, "I don't understand. When I pray to the gods, I always give them something - a garland of flowers, or some food, or the life of an animal. Then they'll be pleased and perhaps hear my prayer. Why is your god different?"

"Our God made the whole earth. He doesn't need our gifts of food and flowers. But he does want one gift from us – our lives."

"What do you mean?"

"God wants us to become his children. He wants us to give our lives over to him. Then we can talk to him any time, like a son or a daughter talks to their father. Ursula doesn't bring you presents when she talks to you, does she? You listen to her because you love her as your child."

Domitia said, "How did you come to hear about this god who is so different from all other gods?"

"I listened to a preacher in the marketplace. This was five years ago, before it became dangerous to speak so openly. He talked about a man called Jesus Christ, who was God's son on earth. Jesus lived and died so that we could become God's children, too."

Crispus told Domitia about all the things Jesus had done – healing sick people and doing miracles. He was crucified like a criminal, but then God raised him to life. Domitia listened intently.

"Why did you never tell me all this before?" she asked him.

"I tried to, but you didn't want to listen. You said Septimus wouldn't approve."

Just for a moment Domitia looked worried. Then she said, "Well, Septimus isn't here now. Tell me some more. I want to know about the God who made Ursula well again."

Crispus said, "If you give your life to God and follow him, you can really know him – not just know *about* him."

"Do you mean I should actually become a Christian?" She seemed taken aback.

"Yes. Does that seem a frightening idea?"

Domitia hesitated. "Well, you know the sort of things people say about Christianity. A secret cult – a weird religion that can alter your mind. And they say that Christians are disloyal to Rome and the Emperor."

This made me angry. "It's not our fault if we have to be secretive," I said. "Our leaders have been arrested. Some of them have been killed. The Emperor hates us, so why should we be loyal to him?"

"Bryn!" Crispus said sharply. "We must obey the Emperor, unless that would mean disobeying God himself. We are to love even the people who hate us, and forgive them when they hurt us."

Domitia stared at him. "No one can really live like that," she said. "It's not natural. I don't think I could ever be a Christian. Anyway, Septimus wouldn't allow it."

Abruptly she changed the subject. "And how was your trip to the village, Bryn? Did you hear any news?"

I felt disappointed. I'd almost thought she was interested... But she'd obviously had enough of talking about God.

IX

ATTACKED

By the end of our third week at the villa, Felix was starting to get restless. He was bored with life in the country.

"Why don't we go back to Rome?" he said. "Just for a visit, I mean? We could go in with the farm cart and come back the next day."

Every week the farm manager sent a cartload of food to the household in Rome. Without this, Septimus and his slaves would have gone hungry.

"Good idea," I said. "But what will your mother think?"

"I won't tell her."

"But if we just disappear, she'll worry," I objected. "You *must* tell her, Felix."

His mother was definitely the worrying type. She was thin, grey and nervous-looking, like a half-starved stray cat.

Her life had been hard. Years ago, her husband and two daughters had been killed in an accident. The building they'd lived in had collapsed – simply fallen in on itself. This was not unknown in Rome. The tall "island" blocks, housing dozens of poor families, were often built carelessly out of cheap materials.

Felix and his mother had been dug out of the wreckage, still alive. Felix was only five at the time; he could barely remember his father and sisters. But he did remember what a struggle his childhood years had been. His mother had had to find work, or they would both have starved. She'd got a job in a laundry, working long hours for little pay. And she'd often gone hungry so that Felix could be fed.

"She keeps telling me I should be grateful to her," Felix would complain. "I am grateful – of course I am, but I wish she wouldn't keep on about it. And then she reminds me that I'm all she has, so I must look after her when she gets old. That's why she got me an apprenticeship. I'd much rather go into the army, or go to sea, or something like that – something exciting."

I sometimes wondered if Felix had become a Christian because he liked the excitement of it. Secret signs, night-time meetings in hidden places, a feeling of danger... He loved all that.

His mother wasn't a Christian. Felix had tried to tell her about God's love, but she always said the same thing. "The gods may love other people, but they don't love me. They've given me a life full of pain and sorrow. They've taken my husband and my daughters, and if I'm not careful they'll take you too, Felix. Then what will become of me?"

Naturally she didn't want Felix to go back to Rome, even if it was only for a day or two. "It's far too dangerous," she said.

"Why? The fire is out, Mother. We'll be perfectly safe. What are you so anxious about?"

"I don't know," she said, helplessly. "I just think it's a bad idea. I wish you would stay here."

But Felix was determined. In the end he persuaded Crispus to come too. This seemed to make his mother feel better about the whole idea. For some reason, she seemed to think Crispus would be able to keep Felix out of trouble.

Two days later we set out for Rome. The ox cart, driven by a slave named Gaius, was loaded up with vegetables and meat. It was a slow journey, for the oxen only travelled at walking pace. We took turns to walk or ride on the back of the cart.

"Where will we spend the night?" Felix asked. "At Septimus' house?" He had never been there, but I'd told him about it. The oxen would be stabled there, ready to leave early next morning.

Crispus hesitated. "I'm not sure. Septimus isn't expecting us. Maybe it would be better to stay with one of the brothers." By *brothers* he meant our Christian friends. I knew that they would give us a far better welcome than his brother-in-law would.

"If any of them still have a home to live in," I said.

By noon, when we stopped to rest from the heat, we could see Rome far away. At this distance it looked the same as always – a vast, white city, spread over hills and valleys like a cloak over a sleeping man.

"I thought the city was supposed to be in ruins," said Felix. He sounded quite disappointed.

Gaius, the driver, grinned. "That's the northern edge of Rome you're looking at," he said. "The fire never reached that far. If you want to see ruins, go into the centre and you'll find plenty."

Before the oxen had time to rest properly, Felix was itching to get moving again. "At this rate we won't get there before nightfall," he muttered.

"True," said Gaius. "But there's no point in getting there too soon. They don't let carts into the city during the daytime."

"But then we won't be able to see anything," Felix complained.

In the end the three of us decided to walk on, leaving Gaius to follow with the ox cart. I thought he looked relieved to see us go. Perhaps he secretly planned to sell some of his cargo on the way to his master's house. I've been a slave myself – I know what slaves get up to.

As we drew nearer to Rome, we noticed something strange. The Campus Martius, a large open space on the edge of the city, was normally used as a training ground for soldiers. Now it was covered in tents, as if a huge army was besieging Rome.

But this was no army. The tents were pitched anywhere and everywhere, and between them, children were playing. Women were stirring pots over open fires. Old people sat, staring aimlessly into space.

"These must be some of the homeless people," said Felix. "Poor things."

"We're homeless too," Crispus reminded him. "It's only thanks to Domitia that we have a roof over our heads."

Looking at the vast encampment, I wondered how people were getting food and water. They didn't appear to be starving, certainly. But there were so many of them... thousands upon thousands.

"Our friends might be somewhere out there," I said.

"How do you plan on finding them, then?" said Felix. "Stand in the middle and shout their names?"

"We could go to the home of anyone we know on the north side of the city," said Crispus. "They might have news of the others."

The only ones we could think of were two women, who were slaves in a senator's house, and old Cassius – and Tiro, of course. I really wanted to see Tiro, to make sure he was all right. What had happened to him after that ride through the fire? Had he got back safely to his master's place in the country?

We decided to call on Tiro first. On our way, we saw signs that normal life was starting up again, at least in this part of Rome. A few shops were open, and market stalls were selling food, although the prices were high.

As we neared the house of Tiro's master, we saw people going in at the front door. Perhaps the master was entertaining friends. That was a good sign – if he was at home then Tiro, his coachman, was probably there too.

We went round to the stable door, and I tapped on it in the usual way – three knocks, pause, then knock again. At first there was no answer, so I tried again.

"Who's there?" Tiro's voice sounded cautious.

"Bryn and Crispus and Felix."

"No one else? You're sure no one else is out there?"

"No," I said, puzzled. "Are you all right, Tiro?"

Slowly he opened the heavy door – and I saw that he was far from all right. He looked as if he'd been in a fight. His dark skin didn't show bruises easily, but one eye was red and swollen, and his mouth was cut.

He also looked frightened. Tiro – frightened? He was one of the bravest people I knew.

"Tiro! What happened?" asked Crispus.

"I got attacked in the street," he said, speaking with difficulty because of his sore lip.

"Were they trying to rob you?" said Felix. "Did they take anything?"

"They weren't thieves, just ordinary men. It was because I'm a Christian," he said. "They hate Christians."

Felix said, "That's nothing new. They've always hated us."

"Not like they do now," said Tiro. "Haven't you heard? People are saying it was Christians who started the fire."

X

THE AFTERMATH

"Come inside," said Tiro. "You don't want to be seen with me, or you'll be in danger too."

He led us into the stables and up some narrow steps to the small room above. This was where he slept, so that he could keep an eye on the horses.

"What happened?" Crispus demanded. "Who did this to you, Tiro?"

"I don't know. There were five or six of them. I'd never seen any of them in my life."

"How did they know you were a Christian?" asked Felix.

"A few of us met together at Cassius' house. I suppose his neighbours know he's a believer. Maybe they saw us arriving, and waited for us to leave, one by one like we always do. Anyway, just as I got to the street corner, they jumped on me."

"Six against one!" said Crispus. "Thank God you're still alive!"

"They weren't planning to kill me. They beat me up, then they left me on Cassius' doorstep for the others to find. It was like a warning. 'Tell your Christian friends this is what's coming to them. This is what they deserve for setting fire to Rome.'"

Suddenly I felt very scared. Of course I had always known it could be dangerous to be a Christian. People had been arrested and even killed. But now, for the first time, a good friend of mine had been attacked...

"Your mother was right," I said to Felix. "It *is* dangerous in Rome."

Crispus said, "Why are people saying that Christians started the fire?"

"Not everyone thinks that," said Felix. "I heard all kinds of rumours when we escaped from the fire. Some people blamed robbers, or the wrath of the gods, or even the Emperor himself."

"Well, things have changed," said Tiro. "Now it's Christians who are getting most of the blame."

Crispus asked again. "Why should people think we would want to destroy Rome? We're not violent. We are supposed to be peacemakers."

"No one knows that, though," I said. "They don't really know much about us. Remember what Domitia said - a secret cult, a weird religion..."

"And don't forget, the Emperor hates us," said Felix. "If he really caused the fire, he's probably looking for someone else to blame. His men could be spreading evil rumours about us. Tiro, you must get out of Rome at once. Now that they know about you, they may come back."

"But I am a slave," said Tiro quietly. "I can't leave unless the master tells me to."

"Aren't you afraid?" Felix asked. He could be very tactless sometimes. I saw Tiro flinch for a moment, as if he was reliving the pain and terror of that sudden attack.

"Of course I'm afraid." He looked at me. "Remember how my horse was afraid to go near the flames? But he knew me, he heard my voice and went where I led him. I can trust God like that. I don't know what lies ahead, but God does, and he will lead me through it."

There was a moment of silence. I suddenly felt glad that I didn't know what the future held – for myself, for Tiro, for any of us. It was better to leave it in God's hands.

Crispus asked if Tiro had news of our friends.

"Most of them escaped from the fire, by God's mercy," said Tiro. "But many are homeless. They're living on the Campus Martius or staying with relatives. I've heard from almost everyone, except for Titus and Livia."

"I saw Titus," said Felix. "It was on the second day of the fire. He was going back into the city to look for Livia. He'd lost her in the crowd."

"But that was almost a month ago," I said.

"If they were still alive, I think someone would have heard from them by now," said Tiro.

We looked at each other. Titus and Livia were both so young; they'd been married for less than a year. Livia had been expecting their first child.

"We shouldn't mourn for them," said Crispus. "They've gone to be with the Lord."

I hated it when Christians said that sort of thing. All right, so death was supposed to be the gateway to heaven – to the city of God. But why shouldn't we feel sad about friends who had died? We would miss them, even if they had gone to a better place than this.

Suddenly I heard a door creak open, and someone shouted up the stairs. "Tiro! You awake? The master wants the carriage to be ready by nightfall."

All of us froze into stillness. Then Tiro shouted back, "All right, I heard you."

The stable door slammed shut, and we relaxed.

"We'd better not stay here," said Crispus. "We mustn't get you into trouble, Tiro."

"And *I* mustn't get *you* into trouble. It's not safe for you to be seen with me," said Tiro.

Before we left, we prayed for each other. Then we said goodbye to Tiro, not knowing when we would see him again.

He let us out by the stable door into the alley. No one was around as we hurried away from the house. When we were safely out of sight of it, we stopped to decide what to do.

Crispus wanted to visit old Cassius, but that might be dangerous. "I promised your mother I'd bring you back safely," he said to Felix. "So I don't think you'd better come to see Cassius. Why don't you and Bryn take a walk for an hour or two? We could meet back here at nightfall."

"Where are we going to spend the night?" I asked.

"I suppose Septimus' house would be the safest place," said Crispus, reluctantly.

We went our separate ways. Felix and I decided to look at the aftermath of the fire. "Much more interesting than going to visit gloomy old Cassius," said Felix. "I want to see all these ruins that people keep talking about."

As he said it, we arrived at a street corner – and came to a sudden stop. It was like reaching a cliff edge, where solid ground turns into emptiness and fallen rubble. Behind us was a normal street. In front of us...

"Oh, Lord!" breathed Felix.

We were staring out across a wasteland. In the valley below us, not a single building was intact. White marble walls had been reduced to blackened heaps of stone. Temples lay in ruin, their columns like dead trees still upright in a burnt forest.

The pattern of streets and squares had been obliterated. I could hardly tell which part of Rome we were looking at. Aqueducts and fountains, marketplaces, palaces... all had vanished. The proud city had become a huge rubbish tip, smelling of death and decay.

"I tried to picture what it would be like," I said. "But I didn't imagine *this*."

"No. Me neither."

Rome had been built over centuries. Six days of fire had destroyed it utterly.

"I don't see how it can ever be rebuilt," Felix said. "It's finished."

XI

THE EMPEROR'S GARDEN

But Felix was wrong. Already the rebuilding had begun.

Down in the valley bottom, I could see men working. There were dozens of them, as busy as ants. They seemed to be clearing the debris.

Walking carefully over the rubble, we went closer to see what was going on. Several gangs of slaves were hard at work under the command of foremen. A large area had already been cleared. At one side was a heap of stones that might be reusable. Everything else – ashes, rubble, scorched brick and twisted metal – was being tipped into ox carts and taken away.

Curious, I asked a foreman where it was all going.

"To the marshes outside the city," he said. "We're filling them in. Maybe that will put a stop to the marsh fever once and for all." Everyone knew that the marsh fever, which killed hundreds each summer, came up out of the swamps.

"What's going to be built here?" Felix asked. But the foreman didn't know – or if he knew, he wasn't saying.

We went on, over a hill and into the next valley. Wherever we looked, work was going on. Then we came to a wall, broken down and smoke-stained. Beyond lay what must once have been an enormous, beautiful garden. Now it was like the site of a bonfire. It had become another camp for homeless people, with children playing under the scorched and shrivelled trees.

"What is this place?" I asked Felix. "I don't remember ever seeing it before."

He said, "It's part of the Emperor's garden. And you never did see it before because it was private, with a huge great wall around it. I wonder if the Emperor knows about all these homeless people living in his garden."

A woman overheard him. "Of course he knows. He offered the use of his gardens to anyone who's home-less. And he's providing food for us all, too. Isn't that amazing? Where would we be without the Emperor?"

Without the Emperor, you might still be safe in your own home, I wanted to say. But I kept my mouth shut.

Felix was less cautious. "Haven't you heard what people are saying about the Emperor? How he ordered the fire to be started?"

The woman looked shocked. "That's a terrible thing to say, young man. The Emperor's own palace got destroyed in the fire. He certainly didn't want it to happen. He's homeless himself now!"

"Oh, yes," said one of the men who was standing around idle at the edge of the camp. "Homeless – except for his summer palace, and all his other houses and estates, and the lands he's taken from his enemies. If that's what homelessness means, I wouldn't complain about it one little bit."

Several other people joined in the argument. Quite a few of them spoke out bitterly against Nero.

"I've heard he's planning to build a golden palace, with grounds that stretch from here to the Capitoline Hill."

"Yes, and it's to have gardens ten times the size of this, with an artificial lake. All built where people like us used to have our homes! It's disgraceful!"

"That's nothing but a rumour," another voice broke in. "Let me tell you the facts. On the day the fire started, I saw some men going round with torches, setting light to things deliberately."

"Yes – the Emperor's men."

"No, *not* the Emperor's men. They were criminals and lunatics belonging to that new religion – Christians, or whatever they call themselves. That's who started the fire."

"It's a lie!" shouted Felix.

By now quite a crowd had gathered around us. The camp was full of people with nothing to do, for the fire had destroyed their usual occupations. I didn't like the look of things. This was the kind of situation where a fight might start.

"Come on, Felix. Let's get out of here," I muttered.

Felix wasn't listening. He had a grim, determined look on his face. "We can't let them go on saying things like that," he said.

"Christians hate our gods. They refuse to worship them," a woman cried out. "They tried to destroy every temple in Rome! They've brought down the wrath of the gods on all of us!"

Felix took a deep breath. He stepped forward into the centre of the group; I hung back at the edge of it, beginning to wish I wasn't there.

"Look at me," Felix said. "I'm a Christian. I never started any fires, and my friends didn't, either. In fact we tried to fight the fire."

It was an incredibly brave thing to do. Also incredibly reckless – but that was Felix all over. For a moment everyone simply stared at him.

"See? I'm not a lunatic or a criminal. I'm just an ordinary person. The only thing that's different about me is that I'm a follower of Jesus Christ. And Jesus taught us to heal people, not harm them – to love other people instead of hating them."

This was crazy! Felix was preaching about Jesus, right there in the Emperor's garden!

"Don't listen to him," the woman yelled. "He's evil. All Christians are evil and they want to destroy us!"

"It's the Emperor who's evil," I cried, but my voice was lost in the shouting.

Some people snatched up stones to use as weapons. Others tried to stop them. There was total chaos. Someone hit Felix, knocking him down, but someone else picked him up. I couldn't get close enough to help him – to tell the truth, I didn't even try. I was far too scared.

"What's going on here?"

The voice was loud and full of authority. I turned to see a troop of soldiers forcing their way through the crowd. As people noticed them, the noise died down, except for the screeching of that crazy woman. "Kill him! Kill the Christian!"

"Somebody shut her up," said the leader of the soldiers. "Now, what happened?"

"It was him. He started it," a man shouted, pointing at Felix.

"He's a troublemaker. He's a Christian. Arrest him!" came other voices. "He deserves to die!"

"I'm not afraid of dying," cried Felix. "You can kill my body, but not my soul. Go on, then, what are you waiting for?"

"There won't be any killing," said the soldier. "Not here, anyway. You're under arrest."

Two of his men grabbed hold of Felix. As they marched him through the crowd, they passed very close to me, but Felix didn't even glance in my direction. Did he despise me for being afraid? Or was he trying not to involve me?

"It's all over. Go back to your tents," the leader ordered, and the people began to move away slowly, reluctantly.

I was the last to move. No one noticed me; no one seemed to remember that I had been with Felix at the start. I was free to go.

But I felt terrible. What should I have done? There was no way I could have saved Felix from being arrested. If I'd stood up for him, I would have been arrested too. That wouldn't have helped anyone.

All the same, I felt I'd let him down. I should have tried harder to make him listen to me. I ought to have dragged him away before he got involved in that argument.

What would happen to him now? When Christians were arrested, the best they could hope for was imprisonment. And Felix would absolutely hate that. He loved action and adventure – he would go mad with boredom if he was locked up.

But far worse things could happen. The Emperor had many ways of dealing with his enemies. Some were crucified. Some were beheaded. Some were put with hungry lions in the arena, hunted down and eaten for the amusement of the crowd.

I suddenly realised that I didn't even know where Felix had been taken. The soldiers had marched westwards – that was all I knew. I tried to follow the direction they'd taken. But I couldn't see where they'd gone, and I didn't dare ask anyone.

Feeling utterly miserable, I made my way back towards the north side of the city. The sun was going down behind the ruined hills of Rome. Broken columns and archways cast long, dismal shadows across my path.

Crispus was waiting on the street corner where we'd agreed to meet. I told him what had happened.

"Oh, no," he said, horrified. "What did Felix think he was doing?"

"I don't know. I tried to stop him... but you know what he's like."

"And how," said Crispus, "are we going to tell his mother?"

XII

A RESTLESS NIGHT

"Maybe Septimus could use his influence to help Felix," I said. "You know – all those important friends he keeps talking about." I mimicked his voice: "'As I was saying to the senator...'"

"He *could*, but I don't suppose he would. He's never even met Felix. And what would he gain by doing it? That's what Septimus always thinks about – what's in it for him," Crispus said. He didn't look hopeful. "But we may as well ask him. I don't know what else we can do, apart from pray."

When we reached Septimus' house, the doorman wouldn't let us in. I knew he recognised us from our previous visit, but he said stiffly, "I'm sorry, I have strict instructions to admit no one unless the master gives permission."

"Please inform the master that his brother-in-law is here," Crispus said, equally stiffly.

The doorman sent another slave with a message. But it was some time before Septimus came to the door. He was far from pleased to see us.

"What are you doing here?" he demanded. "I'm expecting guests tonight. I don't want them to know that I have anything to do with... people of your religion."

"Christians, you mean?" Crispus said, loudly. "You were more welcoming last time we were here, Septimus."

"Shhh!" Septimus looked up and down the street. Fortunately, it was empty. "All right, you can come in."

He led us to a small room, away from the main dining room. Plainly we were not to mix with his important guests.

"Don't you know things have changed since you left Rome?" he said. "It's very dangerous for Christians now. Your people are being blamed for starting the fire. You should have stayed at the villa."

"Yes, we know that," said Crispus, and we told him what had happened to Felix.

"Is there any way...?" Crispus hesitated. "Could you possibly...? I mean, you know a lot of people, Septimus. People with influence. Couldn't you find a way to help Felix?"

"He's only 15," I said. "And he didn't *do* anything. He certainly didn't start the fire or help to spread it. If he gets punished, it will be totally unfair!"

"Fair, unfair... those words used to have some meaning," said Septimus. "But not any more. Their meaning depends on the wishes of the Emperor."

"That's why we must try to get Felix released," said Crispus.

Septimus said, "Well, it's no use coming to *me*. I don't want to be seen giving help to Christians – that would be far too risky for a man in my position. I may have friends in high places, but I have enemies too. They would jump at the chance of putting me in prison."

It was just as Crispus had said. All the same, I couldn't help feeling disappointed.

"And now, I suppose," Septimus went on, "you need a bed for the night. Very well, but I want you both out of here first thing tomorrow. Get out of Rome, go abroad – go where you like, as long as you don't come back here. Understand?"

He turned and swept out of the room. I heard him giving orders to his slaves. They brought us food and drink, but neither of us had much of an appetite. Then they took us to a bedroom.

"Now what?" I said.

"We pray," said Crispus. "You know what happened to Peter when he was arrested in Jerusalem? His friends prayed for him. That night an angel appeared in his prison cell and led him to freedom."

I had often heard this story. Peter was an amazing man – one of Jesus' first followers. He was old now, but he still had clear memories of everything Jesus said and did. His life had been spent telling people about Jesus, all across the empire from Jerusalem to Rome.

Then, last year, he had been arrested again. For months all the Christians in Rome had been praying for him; but no more angels had appeared. At the time of the fire he was still in prison.

Why did God sometimes answer prayers and sometimes not? Of course I wanted to pray for Felix. Of course I believed that God *could* free him... But would he?

We prayed for a long time. Then we talked about what to do next. Someone would have to tell Felix's mother what had happened. But there was no need for both of us to return to the villa. One could go and the other could stay in Rome, trying to find a way of helping Felix.

In the end we decided that Crispus should stay. Not here, obviously: Septimus wouldn't allow that. He might have to camp out among the refugees, or stay with old Cassius. That might be dangerous...

"But not as dangerous as facing Felix's mother," I said. I was absolutely dreading it. She would go mad, I thought – mad with grief and terror.

We could hear drunken laughter from the courtyard. It sounded as if Septimus' guests were leaving. "I hope they had a pleasant evening," said Crispus bitterly.

I wondered what sort of evening Felix had had. Was he enjoying the excitement of being arrested? Somehow I doubted it.

***

I had a restless night. I kept waking up, and every time it happened, the memories of Felix's capture came back to me like a bad dream.

I felt really guilty. Felix was my friend, but I hadn't stood by him when he was surrounded by enemies.

Felix was far braver than I was. He spoke out fearlessly in front of a hostile crowd, while I kept my head down and stayed silent. Surely God must be pleased with Felix and angry with me?

The room felt so hot, it was stifling. I got up and opened a window shutter, but the air that came in was as warm as the room. Along with it came the pale light of dawn and a faint, bitter smell of ashes. I knew Rome would not be rid of that smell until all the debris of the fire had been cleared away.

My movements awakened Crispus. "What's the matter?" he said, drowsily. "Why are you up so early?"

"I can't sleep," I said.

"Are you all right?"

"I keep thinking about yesterday. I shouldn't have been such a coward, especially when Felix was so brave..."

"So foolhardy, you mean." He yawned and sat up in bed. "Remember what Jesus told his disciples? He said, 'I'm sending you out like sheep among wolves. So be as cautious as snakes and as gentle as doves.' That's not how Felix was acting yesterday."

"No," I said. "He wasn't like a sheep or a dove. More like an angry lion."

This made Crispus smile. "Maybe Felix wasn't following God's will, just his own reckless nature. Do you think anyone listened to what he said?"

"No. They were all too angry."

"So there are times when it's right to speak, and times when we should be silent. We have to listen to

God's voice. Then we'll know the right time to speak out."

I thought about this. "But I wasn't listening to God's voice any more than Felix was. I was too frightened to think straight. And now I feel really bad..."

Crispus said, "Did you ever hear what happened to Peter on the night when Jesus was arrested?"

I shook my head.

"Peter followed the soldiers, wanting to see what happened to Jesus. He waited in the courtyard of the building, but a woman recognised him. She said, 'You're one of Jesus' friends, aren't you?' And Peter said, 'No. I've never seen him before in my life.' He was afraid, so he lied to save his own skin. Three times he said it, cursing and swearing: 'I don't know who you're talking about. I've never met him.'"

"Really? Peter did that?" I was amazed.

"Yes, and afterwards he felt even worse than you. He went out alone into the darkness. He didn't think Jesus would ever forgive him."

I said, "But Jesus did forgive him."

"Yes, like he always does, whenever someone is truly sorry for the things they've done. So don't go on feeling guilty, Bryn. If you've done wrong, ask God to forgive you – and he will."

"Lord," I prayed, "I'm sorry I got so frightened yesterday. I forgot to listen for your voice. Please forgive me... And make me braver the next time."

I felt as if a heavy weight had been lifted off my back. I stood at the window. Cool against my face came the breath of the small wind that rises at dawn.

It was sunrise. A new day, a fresh start.

XIII

A DREAM

It didn't seem worth going back to bed. Gaius, the cart driver, would be leaving early to return to the villa. If I wanted to travel with him, I had better get up.

There were slaves already at work, sweeping the vast rooms and corridors. When I asked one of them where to find Gaius, I was told he couldn't go back yet because the ox cart had a broken wheel. Gaius would have to find a wheelwright to mend it. "But the Street of the Wheelwrights was destroyed in the fire," said the slave. "It may take him days to find someone."

Good. That gave me a reason not to go back just yet. I really didn't want to have to tell Felix's mother...

I ordered some breakfast – or rather I didn't *order* it, I asked for it politely. I could never get used to giving orders in the proper manner. The slave smirked at me and went away. I went into the dining room, sat down and waited. Naturally the food didn't arrive for ages.

Just as I started eating, Septimus arrived. He looked terrible – pale and hollow-eyed, as if he'd slept even less than I had. I thought he must have drunk too much the night before.

I greeted him, and he grunted something in reply. Without being told to, a slave brought him bread and honey, but he didn't seem hungry.

Then he said abruptly, "This god you believe in. Does he ever speak to people through dreams?"

"Yes, sometimes he does. I've heard that—"

"I had a dream last night," he said, interrupting me. "In fact I had the same dream over and over. I had to find that friend of yours, Felix, or whatever his name is. I went all through the city, but I kept ending up at the same place – outside a house on the Via Aurelia. I knew the house; I've been to dinner there."

"And you think that's where they've taken Felix?" I said.

"Well, that's what the dream seemed to be telling me. I heard a voice..." At the memory he shivered, as if the voice had scared him somehow – or filled him with awe. "And the voice said, 'Tell Bryn, this is where his friend is.'"

I jumped up. "I've got to tell Crispus about this."

"Wait! What are you going to do?"

"Well, go to the house, of course. Try to get Felix released."

"If you do, they may arrest you too, do you realise? They're trying to round up all the Christians they can find. If they arrest you, they will question you about other Christians. You may end up giving them the names of all your friends."

"No," I said. "I wouldn't tell them anything."

"It's easy to say that now. Did you know that slaves can be questioned under torture?"

The thought filled me with horror. "But I'm not a slave. I was freed two years ago."

"Well, make sure you have proof of that," he said, grimly. "You're British, as anyone can tell whenever you open your mouth. The only Britons in Rome are slaves, or freed slaves. The Emperor's men may assume you're still a slave unless you can prove otherwise."

I touched the leather pouch hanging around my neck, inside my tunic. It was still there, safe.

Septimus noticed what I'd done.

"Even that may not protect you," he said. "Certain people believe they can ignore the law. The house I mentioned – it used to belong to a wealthy man, Mamercus Annaeus Novatus. He made a will leaving half his property to the Emperor. A month later he killed himself, or so people said."

"You mean the Emperor had him murdered?" I said.

"Quiet! It's not safe to speak of these things openly. What I'm trying to say is, be careful. Don't walk boldly into danger, like your friend did."

"I'll try not to," I said. "Thank you for your help."

His eyes hardened again. His voice grew harsh. "And whatever you do, don't mention my name!"

***

"That must be the house," said Crispus. "Don't stop and stare... keep walking."

We had crossed the river Tiber to its western side. This part of the city seemed to have no fire damage: the river must have protected it. We were walking along the Via Aurelia, a main road leading westwards.

We'd found a place that matched Septimus' description: a large house, opposite a fountain and next to a shrine to the goddess Fortune. It showed no windows on the outside. This meant robbers couldn't get in, but also that people inside couldn't get out, except by the front door. And the door was guarded by soldiers.

Just to make sure we'd got the right house, Crispus asked an old man further along the street. Yes, that was the house that used to belong to Mamercus Annaeus Novatus. Now it was owned by the Emperor. His face showed what he was thinking, but didn't dare to say.

"Is it true that Christians are being held prisoner there?" I said.

"So people say." He looked puzzled. "Who are these Christians, anyway? I'd never even heard of them before all this trouble began. But suddenly everyone's talking about them."

Crispus explained about the Christian faith, and he listened, interested. This must be what Crispus meant by "the right time to speak".

"Are you Christians, then?" the old man asked.

"Yes, we are."

Nervously, the old man looked up and down the street. "That's a very dangerous thing to say," he warned us. "A lot of people hate even the word

'Christian'. But you seem harmless enough to me. I must go now. Goodbye!"

He hobbled away without looking back.

I said to Crispus, "We're going to have to talk to those soldiers. What should we do if they ask us the same question – are we Christians?"

"Give the same answer," said Crispus. "What else can we do? Lie about it?"

"I just don't know if I will be brave enough to tell the truth," I said.

"Neither do I," said Crispus quietly. "I'm not a very brave person. Let's pray that God gives us the strength and courage to say what he wants us to say."

So we prayed. Then we talked about what to do.

There was no need for both of us to go to the house and risk being arrested. In the end we decided that Crispus should go. I would watch from a distance to see what happened.

Septimus had given us a bag of money. "You'll get nothing, not even information, unless you pay the guards," he had told us. "And you might want to take some food to your friend. If he's actually there, that is, if the dream spoke truly." He'd still had a haunted look on his face. He would be relieved, I thought, if his dream turned out to be quite meaningless.

By now it was nearly noon, and very hot. The four soldiers on duty were standing under the arch of the front door, trying to get some shade. Crispus approached them humbly and politely. He was carrying some bread, cheese and olives, which we'd bought on the way.

I was pretending to drink at the fountain on the opposite side of the street. I wished I could hear what was being said, but I was too far away. The soldiers didn't seem hostile, though. They looked at the things Crispus was carrying, and one of them, laughing, grabbed a handful of olives.

Crispus asked them something. He handed over some money. The soldiers seemed to be arguing among themselves, but finally they came to an agreement. One of them opened the big front door and escorted Crispus inside.

My heart beat faster. He had got in! I just hoped he would get out again.

There was nothing I could do except wait and keep on praying. I sat on the stone edging of the fountain. Even in the midday heat, I felt cold prickles of fear, as sharp as hailstones. If Crispus got arrested, what could I do? What would happen to Marcella and the children?

Some women had stopped to have a gossip, loud enough for me to overhear. Soon I realised they were talking about the imprisoned Christians.

"They sing in there, can you believe it? I've heard them."

"Ha! They'll sing a different tune if they end up in the arena!" another woman said, and she smiled.

"Yes," said the first woman, rather doubtfully. "Did you go to the last Games? The Christians there were a bit of a let-down, if you ask me. Most of them didn't even seem frightened of dying. I like it when people run around more – try to escape. It's boring if they just stand there like lumps of meat."

I felt sick. Was this what would happen to Felix – and to Crispus too, if he was arrested? Oh, God... Why don't you stop these things from happening?

"Well, I thought the Christians were brave," a third woman said. "I felt sorry for them. I don't want to see any more of them getting killed. Haven't they been punished enough?"

This seemed to anger the others. "Punished enough, when they destroyed half of Rome? Kill them all – they deserve it!"

There was a movement across the street. Crispus came out, followed by the soldier, and the door was locked. I followed Crispus down the street and around a corner.

"Well? Was Felix in there? Is he all right?" I asked as soon as it was safe to talk.

"Yes, he's all right. In fact he's in good spirits. The prisoners are being treated quite well. The guards don't stop them from talking to each other, or praying together."

This was good news. At least Felix wasn't being ill-treated. But I could tell by Crispus' face that there was some bad news to come.

"Tiro's in there too," he said. "And old Cassius. They were both arrested this morning, along with dozens of other people."

"At least they weren't taken to the arena," I said.

"Only because the cells at the arena are already full." His face was grave. "I don't think Nero will call a halt until he's captured every Christian in Rome."

XIV

SIGNED AND SEALED

Septimus, before we left that morning, had asked us to come back and tell him what we found out. "That is if they don't arrest you," he said. "And if they do let you go, make sure you're not followed."

No one seemed to be following us. In fact, the guards hadn't questioned Crispus much – they had only been interested in his money.

"One of them did ask why I wanted to see Felix," said Crispus. "I told them he's my brother. Well, it's true. He *is* my brother, just like Tiro and Cassius and all the other believers."

"Did you get a chance to talk to Tiro?" I asked, anxiously.

"No, only to Felix."

Tiro was the one I was really worried about. When I first arrived as a slave in Rome – alone and frightened, unable to speak a word of the language – Tiro had been my only friend. Because of Tiro, I had become a Christian. And Tiro had set me free from slavery, using money he'd been saving up to buy his own freedom. I owed him so much. I had to help him if I could.

"Do you think, if we paid the guards enough, they'd let one or two people escape?" I said, hopefully.

Crispus shook his head. "I don't think they would ever take such a risk. If the Emperor found out, he'd have them beheaded."

Feeling downcast, we went back to see Septimus. Crispus told him that his dream had been quite accurate. "It must have come from God," he said.

Septimus looked very thoughtful. "This god of yours – is he powerful? More powerful than mighty Jupiter?"

"Yes," said Crispus.

"So if you pray to him, he might rescue his followers from prison."

"Well, yes. Of course we are praying for our friends, but—"

"But many Christians have already been killed. Wasn't anyone praying for them? Or doesn't your god care if his followers die?"

"He does care," said Crispus. "Whether we live or die, he loves us. And so we're not afraid to die, for beyond death lies heaven, where we'll meet with him face to face."

"You really think that you can live after your death?" Suddenly there was a look of longing in Septimus' eyes.

"I know I will, because Jesus promised..."

I felt impatient. We should be doing something to help our friends, not wasting time preaching to Septimus. There was a chance that Domitia might become a Christian – but Septimus? Never. He was a hard-hearted man. Even the healing of his daughter had made no impression on him.

My mind began to wander. I thought of Tiro and what might happen to him. Questioned under torture... He was brave and strong, but that would only make things worse for him. It would mean he lived longer and suffered more.

If he hadn't bought my freedom, he would not be a slave now. He might still have been arrested as a Christian, he might still face death – but he wouldn't be tortured first.

Suddenly I had an idea. I could go to see Tiro's master, Lucius. Tiro had served him well for a long time. Maybe I could persuade him to help.

But would I even be allowed to speak to him? I had left his house in disgrace, a thief caught in the act. Lucius was a just and fair master, but he had no time for slaves who couldn't be trusted. He would probably refuse to see me.

There was only one way to find out.

***

The next morning, feeling so nervous that my palms were sweating, I walked towards the home of my old master.

I wondered if anyone would recognise me. It was more than two years since I'd left the place, and in that time I'd changed a lot. I'd grown taller and stronger. I could speak Latin well. I wasn't the skinny little boy who had arrived here from Britain, knowing nothing, afraid of everyone.

Along with four or five other people, I waited outside Lucius' front door. My old master was rich, and every day he would have visitors asking for help or money. The man beside me had once been a slave of the household. After he had served the master faithfully for ten years, he'd been given his freedom, and he started up a shop selling copper and brassware.

"Doing all right, I was," he told me. "I'd just moved to a new shop near the Circus Maximus. I got in a load of new stock..."

Already I knew what he was going to say. "And it all went up in flames?"

"That's right." He looked defeated. "Now I've got no shop and nothing to sell. I can't start up again without money, can I? Then I thought of the master. Maybe he won't remember me after all this time, but I reckon his secretary will. Pallas will put in a good word for me."

"Don't count on it," said the man next to him. "Pallas is sick with the marsh fever. His assistant is in charge – and he hasn't got a good word for anybody. Theon, his name is."

Theon! I felt as if I'd been punched in the stomach. Theon was an old enemy of mine. He'd always hated me. It was Theon who tracked me down when I stole a carved ivory figure from the master's house. I could still picture his face... that gloating look as he taunted me. "I hope you go to a cruel master, who'll beat some sense into you. That's what you need, you thieving barbarian!"

I might as well leave right away. If Theon had any say in things, I would never get to see Lucius.

But maybe he wouldn't recognise me. After all, it was more than two years since we last met. I could keep my head down, looking humbly at the ground, saying as little as possible... For Tiro's sake, I had to try.

We were kept waiting for a long time. Then we were allowed to go in. I recognised the doorman, but he didn't look twice at me. That was a good sign, I thought.

I didn't know the slave who led us into the atrium. It felt very strange to be back in this house, where I'd spent a year as a slave. The house itself had changed very little; it even smelled the same.

"Stop. Who are you and why do you want to see the master?" Theon's voice hadn't changed much either. He still sounded proud and arrogant.

I didn't look at him. I made my voice as deep as possible and tried not to sound like a Briton. "I'm a friend of Tiro, the coachman. He's been arrested."

"I know that," said Theon impatiently. "What do you want?"

"Maybe his master can help him," I said. "I can tell him where Tiro is."

"Oh, very well. Wait in line."

One by one, we were allowed to talk to the master. At last it was my turn. I said a swift prayer under my breath. Please help me to say the right thing...

Lucius looked at me enquiringly. It was plain that he didn't recognise me. Taking courage, I explained where Tiro was being held, and what might happen to him.

As I was talking, I heard a sudden gasp from Theon. He stepped forward. "Master! Do you know who—"

But Lucius held up a hand to silence him until I'd finished. He gave me a searching look. "Who are you?" he asked me. "I believe I know your face."

"My name is Bryn. I was once a slave in your household." Then I added – before Theon could remind him – "I stole from you. I'm sorry. I know it was wrong to do that."

"Ah yes. I remember now. So why do you think I should listen to you?" His voice was as cold and hard as marble.

"It's not me who needs your help, it's Tiro," I said. "He has served you well, hasn't he? He doesn't deserve to be tortured and killed when he hasn't done anything wrong! You could speak up for him. You could save him."

Lucius thought for a moment. Then he said, "To save him is impossible. He's a Christian, and in the Emperor's eyes all Christians deserve to die. If I try to speak up for him, suspicion will fall on me and on my family. I can't take that risk."

"Then do one thing for him," I said, desperately. "Give him his freedom. If he's a free man, not a slave, he can't be questioned under torture."

Again Lucius was silent. I said, "I can't pay you what he is worth because I don't have enough money. But I could serve you in his place. Take me instead of him, and give him his freedom."

Lucius gave me a scornful look. "How much do you know about horses? You could never replace Tiro. Anyway, I don't want another Christian in my household – that would be asking for trouble. Am I right in supposing that you have become a Christian?"

I nodded silently.

"I don't approve of these foreign cults," Lucius said. "They are popular for a few years, then they die away. Twenty years from now, the name of Christ will be forgotten. Why can't people stay loyal to the gods of Rome, who made our city great?"

There was nothing more I could say. I should never have come here. I should have known it would be useless.

As I turned to go, Lucius said, "Wait. How long has Tiro served me, Theon?"

"I'm afraid I don't know, sir. Let me look it up in the records."

Theon took a scroll from a shelf and unrolled it. It took him a little time to find the answer. "He was purchased ten years ago last month, master – in July."

"Ten years ago in July! Then he should already have been freed. Why didn't Pallas remind me? He knows I usually free my most deserving slaves after ten years' service."

"Er... Last month we had the small matter of the fire," Theon pointed out.

"Yes, yes. Well, we must put this right at once. Make out the document to give him his freedom, Theon. Write the date as it should have been, in July."

Theon wrote busily on a piece of parchment. When he'd finished, the master scanned it carefully. He gave an approving nod. Then he rolled it up, sealed it with wax and marked it with his personal seal ring.

It was done! I could hardly believe it. Tiro might still be imprisoned, but now he was a freedman, not a slave.

Thank you, Lord, I said from the depths of my heart.

XV

THROUGH THE DOOR

Theon led me out of the study. In front of Lucius he had been polite to me, but now I could see how angry he was.

"What are you doing here?" he demanded, in a furious whisper. "How did you get back to Rome?"

"Oh, it's a long story," I said. "You know something, Theon? You tried to hurt me but in the end you helped me. I'm free now, and you're still a slave."

This really maddened him. He looked as if he would like to kill me. I smiled at him, enjoying the moment.

"You'd better get back to work," I reminded him. "Who knows? If you behave yourself, the master may free you in ten years or so." Then I walked out with my head held high.

Maybe you shouldn't have said that, a small voice told me. But I didn't care. I had got what I came for.

I hurried through the city and over the river. I could have gone back to Septimus' house to find Crispus, but I didn't bother. It would only look suspicious if Crispus tried to visit the prisoners again so soon. Better if I did it. Besides, I wanted to see Tiro's face when I gave him the proof of his freedom.

I walked nervously towards the guards at the door. The four soldiers on duty were different from before, but they looked equally bored with the job. They slouched against the wall. This is not what we were trained for, their attitude seemed to say.

"Excuse me," I said. "I have a letter for one of the prisoners."

"So? What do you want us to do about it?" said one of the guards.

"Er... Can I take it to him, please?"

"And why should we let you do that?" said another guard.

"It's very important."

"Yeah – to him, maybe. Not to us," the first one said, grinning.

I fumbled in my money pouch, remembering too late that it was almost empty. It was stupid of me to come straight here, I realised. I should have asked Crispus for some money.

Please, God, help me to get in there, I prayed silently.

"Look out," said one of the soldiers. "Officers on patrol."

The men suddenly straightened up. Instead of slouching, they stood to attention. "Put that money away and clear off," one of them hissed at me.

But I didn't move. Maybe this was my chance to get into the house.

There were two officers – one quite young, the other older and tougher-looking.

"Everything still quiet in there?" the senior man asked.

"Yes, sir. Quiet as mice, they are," a soldier said.

"Except when they sing," said another, pretending to cover his ears.

"How many have we got here?"

"There's 36, sir, not counting the children."

"Is that all? The Emperor needs a hundred of them in three days' time."

The men looked interested. "Is the Emperor planning to hold more Games?"

"No, he's had a new idea. He wants a hundred Christians to light up his gardens at night." The senior officer seemed to enjoy the puzzled looks the men gave him, then he explained, "They're to be covered in tar and set alight. They'll burn to death as a punishment for the burning of Rome."

I must have gasped aloud, for the young officer turned to look at me. Just for a moment, the expression on his face showed me he hated the idea as much as I did.

Burned alive! That was even worse than facing lions in the arena. I couldn't bear the thought of Tiro enduring such pain. And Felix, and Cassius, and all the others in there... They would suffer the worst kind of death, agonising and slow.

What was the point of winning Tiro his freedom? It wouldn't save him from the torture of the flames. In three days he would die, unless we could find some way to rescue him. I must go back and tell Crispus what was going to happen.

My attention had been on the soldiers. Now I looked around, and got a sudden shock. Theon was standing a few paces away, watching me.

What was he doing here? He must have followed me from Lucius' house. And that could only mean trouble.

"Hey, you soldiers," Theon called. "You want some more Christians? There's one standing right next to you. Arrest him!"

I turned to run... but too late. Two soldiers grabbed hold of me.

"Bring him here," said the senior officer. "Well? Is it true? Are you a Christian?"

"Naturally he'll try to deny it," said Theon scornfully.

Oh, yes, I wanted to deny it. I wanted to tell them any lie that might save my life: I don't know what he's talking about. He's making a mistake – he's got the wrong person. I've never seen him in my life before.

But something stopped me. I found a strength and courage that I never knew I had.

"Yes. I am a Christian." My voice, to my surprise, sounded quite steady and calm.

The officer looked amused. "Isn't that convenient? We don't even have to go out looking for them. They just come walking in off the street!"

***

That was how I got into the house. I suppose you could say I got what I prayed for, but not the way I wanted it to happen.

I was shoved inside, and the heavy door thudded shut behind me. I could hear the soldiers laughing. They probably thought I was an idiot, too stupid to understand what would happen if I told the truth. And Theon must be laughing too.

Maybe I *had* been stupid. "Don't walk boldly into danger," Septimus had warned me. But that's exactly what I had done. Oh, God, please help me...

"Bryn!" It was Felix. He looked delighted to see me. "Have you brought us some more food?"

"No. I've been arrested."

I told him what had happened, but I didn't mention what the officer had said. It was too frightening.

"I'm glad you're here," said Felix. "What I mean is, I'm not glad you got captured. But I've had no one to talk to. Everyone here is older than I am – or a lot younger. There are children here too, you know. Whole families have been arrested."

I looked around the large hall of the house, which had been built for a rich man. The pillared walls were painted with scenes from Rome's history, and the floor was covered in bright mosaics.

But now the room looked as crowded as a busy street. People walked around restlessly, or stood together, talking. I recognised some of the faces, although many were strangers. Before the fire there had been several groups of Christians in Rome, all meeting in different houses.

When I saw Tiro, I gave him the little scroll. At first he didn't realise what it was.

"It's your freedom," I said. "Lucius said you should have been freed weeks ago."

"Oh, good," said Felix, sarcastically. "Now Tiro can die a free man instead of a slave. What's the point?"

"If you had ever been a slave," Tiro said to him, "you wouldn't ask that question. Bryn, I can't thank you enough. Was it for this that you were arrested?"

I nodded.

Felix said, "Slave or free, it makes no difference. We're probably all going to die."

"Yes," Tiro said softly. "And then we'll know the true meaning of freedom."

XVI

NOT ME

The meal that evening was a thick stew made from dried lentils and chickpeas.

"Get used to it," said Felix. "It's all there is in the storeroom – the house has been left empty for months. There's no fresh food at all. I shared out what Crispus brought me, but it didn't go far amongst this lot."

There wasn't enough space for all of us in the dining room. Felix, Tiro and I ate at a table in the courtyard, along with a young family. The three children were very quiet, as if they didn't dare to ask questions. They gazed at us with big, frightened eyes.

Would Nero kill us all, even the little ones? Perhaps he would spare the children's lives, but they wouldn't survive for long with no one to look after them. I looked again at their anxious faces. They were too young to understand any of this, and far too young to die.

"There must be some way of getting out of here," I said.

"There is a way," said Felix.

"What? You've found a way out?" I gave him a disbelieving look. "Why are you still here, then?"

"Because there's one small problem. We could get out all right... But we'd probably kill ourselves in the process."

"You've been up on the roof," I guessed. "How?"

"Oh, it wasn't too difficult. Onto the roof of the walkway, then up that angle between those two walls... See?"

It did look possible – for someone young and fit, that is. Small children and old people wouldn't have a chance.

Felix went on, "But I couldn't find a way down on the outside. There are no houses joined on to this one, so it's a two-storey drop on every side. You couldn't jump; you'd need a rope. And I can't find one."

"Did you see how many guards there are?" Tiro asked him.

"Four at the front door, two at the back. It looks like they've barricaded the back door into the stables, but I couldn't see properly. I was afraid to lean out too far."

"The front door isn't barricaded, only locked," I said.

Felix began to get excited. "We could make a battering-ram and knock it down. This place is a private house – it's not built like a fort. I bet we could have the door down in no time at all!"

"No time at all?" I said. "Without the soldiers hearing anything? If you can build a silent battering-ram, you must be very clever, Felix."

"Even if they do hear us, there are only four of them," Felix said. "How many men do we have here? At least fifteen."

"But we don't have any weapons," I objected.

"We'll rush them. We'll sweep them away," said Felix, full of confidence. He'd never been on a battlefield, of course. He had never seen Roman soldiers in action.

I said, "Four armed men could hold that doorway against a hundred of us. It's such a narrow space we would only be able to attack them a few at a time – they'd slaughter us."

"Stop!" said Tiro. "We mustn't talk like this. Fighting, attacking, killing – is this how God wants us to live?"

I stared at him. "Tiro, you don't know what the Emperor has in store for us. It would be better to die by the sword."

"What do you mean?" Felix demanded.

I couldn't tell him – not in front of those listening children. The words stuck in my throat.

"Let's take a walk around the garden," I said.

The garden, enclosed between the house and the stables, was beautiful, though rather overgrown. A statue gazed serenely across a dried-up pool. The cool evening air was filled with the scent of flowers.

There, in that peaceful place, I told Tiro and Felix what the soldiers had said.

"Three days?" asked Felix. All at once he looked very scared. "In three days we'll all be burned alive?"

"You see, Tiro, we have to do something," I said.

"We must pray. That's the most important thing we can do," said Tiro. "And we should tell the others about this. All of us should be praying."

Felix looked at me, and I knew what he was thinking. Pray, yes, of course. But don't just sit around and wait for a miracle that might never come. Do something! Take action!

***

We prayed together – the whole group of us – until late into the night. I remember the prayer of old Cassius. He spoke the same words that Jesus used, the night before he was crucified.

"Father, all things are possible for you. Please take this cup of suffering away from us..."

But Jesus had to drink the cup of suffering right to the bitter end. He was whipped, taunted and spat upon. He was nailed to a cross, hanging there for hours in unimaginable pain. "Why have you abandoned me?" he cried out to God, his Father. And then he died.

Would it be the same for us? Would we have to suffer as Jesus did? It was very hard to pray, as Jesus did, "Not what I want, but what you want, Father."

I knew that after death there would be life... But somehow the thought of heaven seemed to bring little comfort. Heaven was far away, pale as moonshine, vague as a thin, drifting cloud.

I had a bad night's sleep in the big room, which had been the slaves' dormitory. I kept waking up out of the same confused dream. I dreamed I was back in the house of Lucius. I was a slave again, and Theon was making my life a misery. I hated Theon; I wanted to kill him. Given the chance, I would get my revenge on him.

Each time I awoke, I had to put my thoughts straight again. I was no longer the slave of Lucius. I had a new master – and his command was to forgive my enemies, not hate them.

But that was hard, so hard to do...

At last it was morning. I got up slowly, with no appetite for breakfast, which was lentils and chickpeas again.

Felix was already up and about. He joined me in the dining room, where we lay on a luxurious couch to eat our lentil stew. He was full of plans.

"I think we may be able to make a rope!" he told me. "Tiro's been looking around in the stables. There's quite a lot of leather harness, reins and things. All we have to do is knot them together."

I tried to feel some interest in this, although I didn't believe his plan could succeed. "How are you hoping to get out without being seen?"

"Oh, it'll have to be at night, of course. Thankfully it's not full moon at the moment. The alley at the side of the house will be pretty dark. But we really need something to distract the guards' attention. Any ideas?"

"I don't see how we can distract the guards if they're outside and we're in here," I said.

"Don't worry," said Felix confidently. "Leave it to me. I'll think of something."

Suddenly we heard loud voices coming from the hall. Two soldiers strode in.

"Right! Everybody out!" they ordered us. "Line up in the courtyard. The tribune wants to take a look at you."

"Why?" asked Felix. But he got no answer except a spear-shaft in his ribs.

We straggled out into the courtyard, where we were made to stand in line. A dozen soldiers were searching the building, bringing out everyone they could find.

I knew a tribune was a very senior officer. (Why would he be interested in us?) A tall, grim-faced man, he looked at us with disdain and ordered a headcount.

"Thirty-seven, sir."

"Not enough. We've got two days to find some more. I want to question some of these. Maybe they'll give us some names."

He walked along the line, picking people out. "This one. These two..."

Not me. Please, not me, I prayed.

He walked past me, then stopped and turned back. His eyes, sharp and merciless as spears, looked straight into mine.

"This one," he said. "That's enough to start with. Keep the others here – I may need some more if these won't cooperate."

A child whimpered. His mother desperately urged him to be quiet. There was total silence as the soldiers led us away.

XVII

OVER THE EDGE

We were marched indoors and down a long corridor. Here, three of us had to stand waiting, guarded by soldiers. The fourth, an old man, was led into a room by two more soldiers. The tribune went into the room and the door was shut.

I strained my ears to hear what went on in the room. But no sound came out.

They could question me for as long as they liked. They wouldn't get much useful information, because I didn't possess much. Of course I knew the names of the people who used to meet at Crispus' house, but I had no idea where they could be found. Most of them had lived in the area devastated by the fire. Perhaps they'd fled the city; perhaps they were living on the Campus Martius. Perhaps they were dead, or already under arrest.

I didn't even know where Crispus would be right now. He might still be at Septimus' house, or making his way back to the villa in the country. I must try to forget the name of Crispus, try to forget about Marcella and the children. Keep silent; don't even think about them. Just forget...

At last the door opened. A soldier escorted the old man out. He didn't look at us as he was taken away down the corridor.

Now it was my turn. I was shoved into the room, which turned out to be a bathhouse. It was very grand, with a large pool, almost full of water. I thought it was an odd place to choose for questioning prisoners.

"Come here."

The tribune was waiting near the edge of the pool. I had to stand in front of him, a soldier on either side of me, while he stared at me in silence. I tried not to look as frightened as I felt.

"Name?"

"Bryn."

"Name of your owner?"

"I'm not a slave." Despite my efforts to stay calm, my voice was shaking. "I was freed two years ago."

He grinned. "Don't be so frightened, boy. Maybe we can help each other. You see, I need a few more Christians. The Emperor has ordered it. You can help me by giving me some names – five, shall we say? Then, if I manage to arrest them, I'll let you go."

When I didn't answer, he said, "Don't you understand? Five names, that's all. Then you can go free. Otherwise, do you know what will happen? You'll be burned alive. You'll become a human torch to light up the Emperor's garden."

A thought slid into my mind: You could give them Theon's name.

Why not? It would only be fair. Theon got me arrested, I would get him arrested. Yes! He would have the fright of his life!

Of course he would deny that he was a Christian. But they wouldn't want to believe him. He was a slave, so they could question him under torture... I felt my smouldering hatred blaze up, fierce and scorching, as if a furnace door had been opened.

The tribune must have seen a change in my face. He leaned forward. "Yes? You're willing to help us?"

He gave me a smile that was meant to look kindly. It was more like the bared fangs of a wolf.

Like sheep among wolves... You must be as cautious as snakes and gentle as doves...

The words came to me so clearly, I almost looked round to see who had spoken. But I tried to ignore them. I didn't want to be a sheep among wolves, helpless against my enemies. I wanted to fight back.

Love your enemies; do good to those who hate you.

Again I tried to push the thought away. Taking revenge on Theon was the exact opposite to what Jesus had said.

Just then there was a hurried knock at the door, and a soldier came in. I recognised him – the young officer who was there when I was arrested.

"You're late, Tullius," the tribune snapped.

"I came as soon as I got your orders, sir," he said.

"Very well. Prepare a wax tablet. Our friend here is about to give us some information."

Tullius smoothed out a wax tablet, ready to write. The tribune looked at me expectantly.

I saw that there was a choice to make. Love or hate; revenge or forgiveness; obeying God or obeying men...

All at once I made my decision. I shook my head. "No. I can't tell you anything."

"What?" The wolfish smile twisted into a snarl.

"I can't tell you any names."

"Oh, I think you can. You were about to say something, weren't you?" He gripped me by the arms and shook me until I was so dizzy, I could hardly stand up. "*Weren't* you?"

When I stayed silent, he motioned to the soldiers on either side of me. "Wash his face for him. See if that refreshes his memory."

I didn't even have time to protest. The two soldiers grabbed me and forced me down on the floor at the edge of the pool. They pushed me forwards until my head and shoulders were over the edge. And then they shoved my head underwater.

It was terrifying. I struggled and thrashed about, but I couldn't get my head above the surface. The soldiers were too strong. I felt my breath giving out. I was desperate to breathe in, but there was no air – no air –

Then they hauled me out. I lay on the floor, coughing and spluttering, helpless as a fish out of water.

"Names," said the tribune. "You were going to give me some names. Or would you rather go swimming again?"

He saw that I was trying to speak. Smiling that smile again, he waited until I had enough breath.

"You can't do this," I gasped. "It's against the law. I'm not a slave."

"I'm afraid I can't quite make out what he's saying. Put him back in!"

"No!" I cried.

Desperately I reached for my money pouch. It wasn't there. It could have fallen in the water... I could have lost it hours ago...

"I need some names," he said, leaning forward. "Not much to ask, is it? A few names to keep the Emperor happy?"

I didn't answer. He waited for a moment, then signalled to the soldiers again.

This time I was better prepared. Before they shoved my face underwater, I took a deep breath and held it. I told myself to keep still, without struggling. But that was impossible. I couldn't control my own panic-stricken body as the last of my air ran out.

Oh, God... help me...

They dragged me out again. Lying sprawled on the tiles, coughing up the water I'd swallowed, I was dimly aware of voices above me.

"...Against the law, sir, if it's true that he's not a slave."

"Oh, don't be so soft, Tullius. You're like an old woman." The tribune sneered. "We're not torturing him, we're bathing him. Emperor's orders. All Christians to get a good wash before they die."

The soldiers laughed.

Tullius said, "Sir, do you think the Emperor's actions are wise? He intends everyone to hate these Christians, but actually the opposite is happening. People are beginning to feel sorry for them, especially when they go bravely to meet with death."

"Are you a soldier, Tullius, or a politician?" The tribune's voice was as cold as a winter night.

"A soldier, sir."

"Then don't question the Emperor's orders. Just obey them. Or do you want to become like our young friend here – an enemy of Rome?"

"No sir."

"Shut up, then. Back to business. Let's rinse him again. Unless he's ready to tell us anything? No?"

Once more they dragged me to the edge. Once more the water closed over my head.

Oh God... I can't take much more of this... Please help me...

I had no more air left inside me. Mustn't breathe in. Mustn't breathe in. But the pain in my chest was so bad that I had to. I choked as the water rushed down my throat. And still they held me under.

That was when everything turned black. Sounds faded away. I couldn't feel the water around me, or the frantic beat of my own heart. All the pain was gone, but not the fear. I was lost in darkness and emptiness.

But then, in the darkness, a door opened. And through the door came light and music, glory, a song of incredible joy... I saw a golden city and sea shining like glass...

I would have run towards the door, but there were hands pulling me back and voices shouting.

"You idiots! You've overdone it!"

"Not my fault, sir! He just seemed to give up all of a sudden."

I opened my eyes. I was back in the bathhouse.

"I think he's still alive, sir!" cried one of the men.

"You'd better hope he is, soldier. The Emperor wants live cattle, not dead meat."

Someone tried to lift me. Someone else thumped me on the back. My stomach heaved, and I was sick.

"He's useless. Get him out of here," said the tribune in a voice of disgust. "And bring in the next one. Come on! We haven't got all day!"

XVIII

THE SMELL OF SMOKE

Before midday, the tribune pulled his troops out of the house, leaving the usual guards outside the door. Perhaps he had got the information he needed.

When I was sure they'd gone, I crept back to the baths. I still felt shaky, and my arms were bruised and sore. But I had to look for my money pouch. I found it lying in a corner. The few coins that had been inside it were gone, probably stolen by a soldier. Not that I cared about the money. My documents were still there – that was what mattered.

I spent that afternoon sitting quietly in the garden, thinking about what had happened. Again and again I tried to relive those few moments... to hear that music again and see the glorious, golden light. The memory of it made everything around me seem shadowy, like twilight.

Had I imagined it, or had I really been given a glimpse of heaven? I tried to tell Tiro about it, but I couldn't find words to describe it.

"Maybe it was a vision," said Tiro. "A kind of waking dream."

I said, "Often I've tried to imagine what heaven is like, but I just couldn't picture it. I'm sure I didn't imagine this... I saw it."

Tiro was skilfully plaiting a rope out of lengths of rein. It wasn't an easy job; the rope would have to be much longer than a rein, and also much stronger. For Felix was still planning his escape bid. He roamed around the house like a hunting-dog seeking out a trail. Every now and then he came back to check on Tiro's progress.

"Will the rope be ready for tonight?" he asked, anxiously.

"I think so. How are you going to anchor it?"

"I'll tie it around a chimney or something."

"You're really planning to escape tonight?" I said.

"We've only got tonight and tomorrow night. After that, the three days will be up." He looked at me more closely. "What's the matter with you, Bryn? Don't you want to get out of here?"

I did want to get out. But I had lost the desperate anxiety of the day before. I'd come close to dying, and now the fear of death was gone. Whatever lay in wait for me, I knew that heaven would be worth it.

***

In the evening, a dozen more captives arrived. One of them, I saw to my dismay, was Crispus.

He told us he'd been arrested at the home of a woman called Caecilia, the wife of a senator. "Septimus suggested I should go to her for help. He'd heard rumours that she was a Christian, and he thought she might ask her husband to use his influence. But while I was there, the soldiers came. They arrested Caecilia and most of her household, as well as me."

"Who told them about her? Was it Septimus?" I demanded. "I always knew he wasn't to be trusted."

Crispus shook his head. "From what the soldiers said, I think it was someone here who betrayed her – one of the prisoners."

I thought of the old man who'd been questioned earlier. He came out of the room with his head down, as if he was ashamed. He wouldn't look at the rest of us.

"It certainly wasn't Septimus," Crispus went on. "You may not believe this, but Septimus isn't far from God's kingdom."

I stared at him. "What makes you say that?"

"That dream of his really made him think. He wants to know more about God. We talked for ages last night. You know Septimus always had one aim in life: to be rich and important. That's all he ever wanted. He managed to do it; but now, he says, it all feels empty."

He stopped suddenly. Everyone in the hall had heard the same noise – a terrified scream.

A woman came running in. "Fire!" she yelled, panic in her voice. "The kitchen's on fire!"

Instantly, fear swept through the hall. We could all remember too clearly the last time we heard that cry of "fire".

Women looked frantically for their children. Some people ran to the front door and began to pound on it, shouting to the guards outside. "Help! Fire! Let us out!"

Tiro and I ran out into the courtyard. The kitchen was on the left-hand side. Great clouds of smoke came billowing from its doorway, along with a smell that I remembered and hated.

"We must put it out. The next room is full of wood and charcoal. If that catches alight..." said Tiro, grimly.

The house had its own water supply, but the pipes ran to the kitchen. The only other water I could think of was in the bathhouse. What could we fetch it in? Pots and jars – but they were in the kitchen too.

We ran back into the hall. My eye fell on two big ornamental vases; Tiro and I grabbed one each. We filled them from the pool and struggled across the courtyard with them. Standing in the doorway, blinded and choked by smoke, we emptied them towards the fire.

Apart from a huge hissing sound, it seemed to make no difference. "We need more people," I gasped. "I'll go."

Everyone was milling about in the passage near the front door. Some people were shouting for help; others prayed quietly. Children cried in their mothers' arms. It was chaos.

"Help us put the fire out!" I shouted, but no one seemed to hear me.

"Silence!" yelled a big man named Micah. "I must talk to the guards. Silence, everybody!"

The noise died down slightly.

"Guards, can you hear me?" he shouted in a voice as big as he was. "Let us out! The house is on fire!"

"Now's our chance," said a voice in my ear. It was Felix. "Let's get going – I've got the rope. This is the best chance we'll ever get."

I looked round. "What about all the others? We can't just leave them here to burn!"

"Burn today or in two days' time – what's the difference?" said Felix impatiently. "Come on!"

"No. Not yet. Help us put the fire out, Felix. Then maybe no one will get burned."

Micah was still shouting at the guards. "If you let us die, the Emperor will kill you! He wants us alive!"

But the door didn't open. We could hear the guards arguing outside.

"Fetch reinforcements!"

"There's no time. We should open the door."

"Are you crazy? Tell the tribune. He'll know what to do."

Then Tiro came in. "The fire's spreading," he yelled. "Women and children – into the garden. Men – help us fetch water. Don't just stand there! Get a move on!"

They hadn't listened to me, but they listened to Tiro. A stream of people followed him.

The sky was almost dark by now, but flames lit up the courtyard. Women hurried their children through a passage to the shadows of the garden beyond. It looked safe there at the moment, but the garden was surrounded by buildings. If they all caught fire...

The men lined up to form a chain across the courtyard. Using whatever containers we could find, we carried water from the pool to the kitchen. I found myself standing next to Felix, just like on that terrible night in July.

"You didn't make a run for it, then?" I said.

"As you said – no, not yet."

Now that people were doing something useful, their panic had lessened. We worked swiftly, and while we worked we prayed.

Oh, Father, if I'm to die tonight, I am ready. But please save the children... Help them to get out safely...

"This is no use," panted the man behind me. "The fire's gaining on us."

By now the room next to the kitchen – the firewood store – was ablaze. Fortunately it was a calm, still night, with no wind to fan the flames. But they were still spreading.

"We need more men," said Felix.

"There aren't any. Everyone's here."

Then I heard the tramp of feet. The courtyard filled with soldiers. The tribune was in the lead, shouting out orders to his second-in-command.

"Take three men and rouse the entire street. We need every able-bodied man to carry water. Set up a chain from the fountain opposite. Do you want to see the whole of Rome in flames again? Then move, man!"

"Yes, sir."

"Right. I want all the prisoners rounded up and locked in the stables. Count them. Put a guard on the door. If a single one of them escapes, you'll be sorry."

Felix shot me a despairing glance.

"You see? We should have left when I said," he muttered. "It's too late now. We've missed our chance."

XIX

A CHANCE

The soldiers formed a row, spears at the ready.

"Don't lock us in!" shouted Micah. "If the fire spreads to the stables, we'll be trapped!"

"No need to panic," the tribune said. "I'll make sure you don't die... not just yet, anyway. Now get going."

The line of soldiers herded us towards the passageway that led to the garden. It looked very dark out there.

"Maybe we do still have a chance," I whispered to Felix.

He nodded. "Make a break to the right as soon as you reach the garden."

Felix and I were among the first go through the passage. The soldiers were well behind us, at the back of the group. They didn't spot us slipping between the columns of the walkway that ran all around the garden.

Everyone else was driven towards the stables. Apart from the red glow that lit the sky behind us, there was no light in the garden. A soldier tripped and fell, swearing loudly.

One of the men was sent back to the house to fetch some lights. He passed within arm's length of us without noticing. But soon he would be back...

"Quick," hissed Felix. "Get up on the roof."

A climbing plant gave us some footholds. We scrambled onto the roof of the walkway. The soldier returned, carrying a blazing branch, which made light and shadows leap around him. By then we were lying flat, out of sight.

We saw the prisoners, including the women and children, file into the stables. "Are the soldiers doing a head count?" I whispered.

"Don't think so. They must have forgotten – just as well for us, eh?"

The soldiers closed the stable doors and fastened them shut with a heavy bar of wood. Then, leaving two men on guard, they hurried back to the house.

"Felix," I muttered, "how are we going to get up onto the roof of the house? If those guards at the stables look up, they'll see us."

"No they won't. The light won't reach that far... At least I hope not."

Everything was now silent in the garden. From the courtyard we could hear shouted orders, hurrying feet, and the hiss and crackle of the flames.

Then I heard a new sound. It came from the stables, wavering at first but growing stronger. The prisoners were singing a hymn of praise to God.

"Good," said Felix. "The louder they sing, the less the guards will be able to hear us. Come on – this way."

We crawled along the roof of the walkway, making for a corner of the garden. It was as far away as possible from the soldiers guarding the stables. When we got there, Felix cautiously stood up. He was right; the guards didn't see him. They were in the light while he was in the shadows.

I watched him climb the wall, using ledges and windowsills, until he swung himself up onto the roof of the house. Then I followed. There was a nasty moment when my foot slipped, but I gripped tightly with both hands and managed not to fall.

Keeping low, we climbed up the sloping tiles and over the peak of the roof. Now we felt safer – no one could see us except from rooftop level. The tiles sloped away beneath us, into darkness.

"What's down below?" I whispered.

"An alley between this house and next door. Hold on, I'll get the rope ready." He uncoiled it from around his waist and looked for a place to anchor it.

Suddenly my heart stood still. Further along the roof, something was moving. I clutched Felix by the arm and pointed silently. He saw it too; a dark figure creeping towards us.

Then a burst of sparks flew up into the sky, lighting up the scene. I almost laughed aloud – for it was Tiro.

"How did you get here?" I asked him as he drew near.

"The same way as you did, but further along. Listen – I've had an idea. There may be a way of getting everyone else out."

We stared at him. "You mean by the back door?" said Felix.

"Yes. It leads into the stables."

"But it's blocked up, and there are guards outside."

"Only two guards," Tiro said. "There are three of us."

"What? The three of us against two armed soldiers?" said Felix. "You're crazy. We wouldn't have a hope!"

"He's right, Tiro," I said, reluctantly. "We'd only end up getting captured again."

"Or killed," said Felix.

There was moment's silence.

"Come on, we're wasting time," Felix muttered. "Let's get out of here."

Tiro turned away without a word. He began to go back along the roof in the direction of the stables.

"Tiro, stop! You can't possibly rescue them on your own!" I set off after him. "Wait. I'm coming."

After a short distance, I looked back. It was all right – Felix was following us. We needed him. He had the rope.

Were we throwing away a God-given chance to escape? Or were we doing what God would want us to do: trying to save others, not just ourselves? I had no idea. All I knew was that I couldn't watch Tiro go into danger alone.

We turned a corner. Now we were on the flat roof of the stable wing. We must be very cautious, for there were guards at the front and back of the building. Any noise would give the whole game away.

But thankfully, our friends were still singing. The words drifted up to us. I thought I could make out Crispus' voice; the song was a psalm that he loved.

Even if I go through the deepest darkness,
I will not be afraid, Lord.
For you are with me.
Your shepherd's rod and staff protect me.

Tiro lay down on his stomach and crawled to the edge of the roof. He was looking down at the rear of the building. After a moment he beckoned us to join him.

There was a long drop to the alley below. On the far side was the blank wall of another large house. The alley was deserted, apart from the two guards, who were standing almost beneath us. We could see them clearly in the light of a burning torch mounted on the wall.

They weren't the most disciplined soldiers I had ever seen – far from it. Their spears were propped against the wall, and one had taken off his helmet. They seemed to be having an argument.

"What's going on in there? No one ever tells us. Stick us round the back and forget about us, that's what they always do."

"When we go off duty we'll find out what happened."

"Yes, when it's too late. When we've missed all the action."

"What action? A few Christians having a singsong? You don't know you're born. When you've fought the German tribes, like I have, you can start talking about action..."

"Oh, shut up. Hey, can you smell smoke? What's going on?"

He paced up and down. Suddenly he said, "I'm going to find out what's happening."

"If old Wolf-head finds out you left your post, you'll be in for it."

"Who'll tell him? I'll be back before you know I've gone." He hurried off along the street and round the corner.

"Quick," hissed Felix. "We need to get down there now. While it's three against one."

There wasn't time to discuss it. Felix hastily uncoiled the rope and looked around for something to hitch it to. But there were no chimney stacks or pillars here, just the flat roof.

"I'll hold the rope," Tiro whispered. "I can take your weight all right."

"Yes, but how will you get down?" I asked.

"Come on! Hurry!" Felix urged us. "Further along – away from the light."

He let down the rope over the edge of the roof. There was no reaction from below.

"Right. I'll go first," he whispered. "Bryn, you follow me as soon as I reach the ground. We'll creep up behind the guard, overpower him... Are you ready?"

Tiro took a firm grip of the rope, winding it around his hands. He stepped back and braced himself as Felix prepared to make his descent. I peered over the edge of the roof. The guard was standing in the circle of light by the doorway, facing away from us.

Felix slid backwards over the edge. He began to climb down the rope.

This was the moment when the guard decided to patrol the alley. Felix heard his footsteps approaching, and froze in position. He didn't make a sound. But the rope still hung down below him. The guard must have walked right into it.

He let out a startled cry, and drew his sword. Felix frantically tried to climb back up.

"Pull him up again, quickly!" I hissed to Tiro.

Too late – Felix had lost his grip on the rope. He fell into the darkness.

XX

HUNTED

Felix landed hard, with a thud and a clatter of metal. I gazed down, straining my eyes and ears. But I couldn't make out a sound or a movement in the dark alley below.

Had the soldier attacked Felix? I thought I could see someone lying on the ground, a shadowy, dark shape. Then there was a groaning noise. I wished our friends would stop singing for a moment.

"What happened?" whispered Tiro, joining me at the edge.

"I don't know. Shhh..."

The dark shape moved. Part of it detached itself and crawled towards the base of the wall. I heard that groaning sound again.

"Where did the guard go?"

"No idea. Unless that's him lying on the ground. Maybe Felix fell on top of him."

"Felix!" Tiro called softly.

We heard an answering moan from below.

"Are you all right?"

"No. My foot... And I think I've killed the guard."

Hastily I climbed down the rope. I found Felix trying to stand up. He had hurt his foot quite badly. Close by, the soldier lay motionless, but still breathing.

"You haven't killed him, just knocked him out," I told Felix. "Tiro! Come down!"

Then I remembered Tiro had no one to hold the rope for him. I ran alongside the wall, looking for a place where he might climb down. Above the doorway I spotted a ledge.

Tiro let himself hang by his arms at full stretch. He dropped lightly onto the ledge. The stones of the archway gave him footholds; he climbed down until he could jump to the ground. Felix came limping along to join us.

The huge double doors – wide enough for a carriage and horses – were blocked with a heavy tree trunk. The three of us struggled to lift even one end of it.

"Oh, come on. Come on. We can't fail now!" Felix gasped.

"All together," said Tiro. "One, two, three..."

Little by little, we shifted the barrier away from the wall at a narrow angle. We couldn't move it very far..

"See if you can open one of the doors now," whispered Tiro.

"What if they're locked?"

Please, God... please, God... Squeezing between the tree trunk and the nearest door, I tried the handle. And the door opened.

The flame of the wall torch lit up startled faces, pale in the darkness of the stables. The singing faltered.

"Don't be afraid. We've come to get you out of here," I said quietly. "Keep on singing!" The guards in the garden might be suspicious of sudden silence.

The song carried on. Everyone was staring at me.

"Doesn't anyone want to come out?" I asked.

For a moment no one moved. Then the disbelieving faces suddenly became hopeful. A woman with a child was the first to come out, blinking in the light. I heard the child say, "Mother, is that an angel?"

"Get away from here quickly," Tiro told her. "Come on, Bryn! Get the others out!"

More people began to squeeze out through the narrow opening. I wondered how long we had before the other guard returned. "Hurry - hurry," I urged them.

"But where are we to go?" the first woman was asking. "We can't go back home. They know where we live."

"Get out of the city," said Tiro. "Go to Ostia, go to Nepeta - anywhere will be safer than Rome. May God guide you... Now go!"

The woman stumbled off down the dark alley. Others followed her, looking bewildered by their sudden freedom. "Don't all go the same way," Tiro told them. "Stay in the back streets. And keep moving. We haven't much time."

The stables were emptying. The song died away. I was afraid the guards at the other door would hear voices or footsteps.

Then the big man, Micah, seemed to go crazy. He started yelling and banging on the door that led to the gardens.

"Hey! Let us out! You can't keep us locked up like this!"

"What's he doing?" gasped Felix.

"Shhh. He's distracting the guards so they don't hear us."

Crispus was among the last to leave the stable. I grabbed his arm. "Tell Micah to come out now."

"He won't," said Crispus. "He volunteered to stay there until the last possible moment. That will give everyone else more time to get away."

It was an incredibly brave thing to do. He wouldn't have time to make his own escape.

"I demand to see your leader!" Micah shouted, still hammering on the door.

"Shut your mouth!" roared one of the guards. "Or do you want us to shut it for you?"

"Come on," said Tiro. "Our job is done. Let's get away while we still can."

We set off at a run – but Felix let out a cry of pain. His injured foot had given way underneath him. He collapsed on the ground, clutching his ankle.

"Go on," he said through gritted teeth. "Don't wait for me. I'll only slow you down."

Tiro and Crispus didn't waste time arguing with him. They stood on either side of him and lifted him up. Then, with his arms around their shoulders, they were able to help him hobble along.

"Make for the edge of the city," said Tiro. "It can't be that far away."

"Yes, but which direction?"

We had come to a place where the alley branched in two. None of us knew this area of Rome. It would be easy to get lost in the maze of back streets between the main road and the river.

"This way, I think," said Crispus, sounding far from sure.

I turned to look back. In the distance I could see the light that burned by the stable doors. Then, suddenly, there were more lights – flaming torches, which shone on spears and helmets. More and more soldiers spilled out into the alley.

We hurried on – if it could be called hurrying. Felix was being as brave as he could, but moans of pain kept escaping from him.

The darkness helped us, and the unlit streets. The soldiers wouldn't be able to see us unless they were almost on top of us. How long could we stay ahead? Micah had bought us some extra time... but maybe not enough.

We came to a crossroads. Which way – which way? At random, Crispus chose a narrow street, which twisted off to the left. Looking back, I saw lights moving at the crossroads. The hunt was drawing closer.

Then we heard triumphant shouts and the shriek of a terrified woman. "They've found someone," Felix muttered.

"That won't hold them up for long," said Tiro, grimly.

We were in a narrow street between tall buildings. A few people, hearing the shouts, came to look down from their balconies. One or two of them cheered us on. Others called out to the soldiers, "Hey, this way!"

"Leave me," Felix gasped. "There's no need for all of you to get caught."

"No," said Tiro, stubbornly. "We're not leaving you."

Crispus and Tiro staggered on. Felix sounded exhausted. His breath came in great gulps that were more like sobs.

Oh, God... why did you let us escape, only to be captured again? Help us!

Another crossroads lay ahead. And suddenly an idea came to me. Felix was quite right - there was no need for all four of us to be taken.

"Listen," I said. "You three go to the right. I'll make sure they see me, then I'll lead them off to the left. I can outrun them. Go on! Now!"

"God go with you, Bryn," said Tiro.

Willing the others on, I crouched in a dark doorway. I could hear rapid footsteps coming closer. This had to be timed just right... not too soon, not too late...

Like a startled hare, I leapt out almost under the noses of the hunters.

"There's one! After him!"

I ran down the street to the left. Heavy feet came pounding after me. Don't get too far ahead, I reminded myself. Keep them following - lead them away from the others.

Twisting and turning through the narrow streets, I started to lose my sense of direction. And the darkness wasn't helping me now. I stumbled several times on cobbles and kerbstones. Once I fell flat on my face, getting up again just in time.

This was getting too risky. It was time to lose my pursuers.

Putting on speed, I raced down a side street. At the bottom there was a choice of three ways. I dived to the right down a narrow, slit-like alley, and was round the corner before the soldiers were anywhere near.

Behind me I heard a confusion of shouting.

"Which way did he go?"

"Don't tell me you've lost him!"

"He can't be far away. We're almost at the river."

"We'll have to split up. You go to the left – you two, straight on – I'll take the right. Shout if you see him."

Not much chance of that, I thought, grinning to myself. I ran on between high walls and shuttered doorways, round another corner – and all at once I stopped.

The alley was a dead end. It led nowhere, except to the river. The moon glinted on deep, dark, swift-flowing water.

For a moment I thought of jumping in. But I could not do it. I couldn't face again that moment when breath gives out and water rushes in, and your chest seems to explode with pain.

Even if I go through the deepest darkness, I will not be afraid, Lord, for you are with me.

I am in your hands, Lord, whether I live or die...

The sound of footsteps echoed hollow between the high stone walls. The hunt was closing in.

XXI

Coming Home

The soldier held a sword in one hand, a flaring torch in the other. He was alone. For an instant I weighed up my chances if I tried to dodge past him. But the alley was so narrow...

"Don't try anything stupid, boy," he warned me.

As he came nearer, I recognised the lean face and watchful dark eyes. It was Tullius, the young officer who had tried to argue with the tribune.

"Ha! Caught like a rat in a trap!" he said mockingly. "But a rat would have had the courage to try and swim for it."

"Not this one," I said. "Even a rat wouldn't risk drowning twice in one day."

I saw that he remembered me. For a moment his face looked troubled. Then, sheathing his sword in one swift movement, he grabbed me by the arm.

"So you thought you could play games with us, did you? Run rings around us and then disappear?"

"I wasn't playing games," I said. "I was helping my friends to get away."

"You Christians are a strange lot," he said, half-scornful and half-admiring. "Weak, yet sometimes brave. You won't stand up and fight, but you're ready to give yourself up for the sake of your friends."

"Yes, well, you wouldn't understand. Our leader died to save other people. Your leader kills other people to save himself."

"That's dangerous talk," he said. "If I were you, I think I would keep my mouth shut. Now get moving." He began to march me back up the alley.

Oh, God... give me the right words to say...

"You're a soldier. Why are you doing the Emperor's dirty work?" I asked him.

"I don't serve Nero. I serve Rome," he said, curtly.

"But Nero's destroying Rome! He burned down half the city!"

Tullius didn't answer. His grip on my arm tightened until it hurt.

"It's true though. Isn't it?" I said. "The flames were spread by soldiers acting on Nero's orders. Was that what you joined the army for – to attack your own city? To kill Roman citizens? To take orders from a madman who thinks he's a god?"

His footsteps slowed.

"I joined the army because my father was a soldier. He told me a soldier's life was an honourable one. But it isn't. Not any more."

"Then why don't you leave?"

"Because I made a promise." His voice was bitter. "And because things may change. The Emperor can't live forever..."

I said, "Nero could rule for another 30 years. The new Emperor might be just as bad, or even worse."

"Not worse. That's impossible," Tullius muttered under his breath. "But the empire will survive. Rome will be great again."

"Jesus said that in the end, all human empires will be swept away. There's only one kingdom that will last for ever - the kingdom of God."

He came to a stop and turned towards me. The burning branch lit one side of his face, leaving the other side in shadow. I couldn't guess what he was thinking.

He said slowly, "I would like to hear more about this. I've grown sick of obeying evil men and killing good ones. But not now. There isn't time."

Just around the corner, I heard the other soldiers talking.

"Any luck?"

"No. He must have got away. Where's Tullius got to?"

In a low voice, the officer said, "I'm going to forget I ever saw you. Try to keep out of sight until daybreak. The search should be called off by then."

I couldn't quite believe it. He was letting me go!

"Thank you," I whispered. "I'll pray for you."

I don't know if he heard me. He turned away and marched around the corner, becoming a soldier again.

"Well? Anyone see anything?" I heard him call to his men.

"No, sir."

"Then what are you standing around for? There are plenty of other fish to catch. Get going!"

***

All that night I crouched in a doorway near the river. Every sound set me on edge. The creak of mooring ropes... the scurry of a rat... voices shouting in the distance... But no one came near.

Where should I go when morning came? Tiro had told people to leave the city. Perhaps I should make for the country villa. That would be where Crispus would go, if he had managed to get away. I only hoped I could remember how to get there.

When the sun came up and the city awoke, I got up cautiously. I walked through the streets, trying to appear ordinary and unafraid. There were soldiers on the bridge as I crossed it, but they didn't even look at me. I was just one more person in the crowd.

The villa was 15 miles away. It would take most of the day to walk there, and I was already exhausted. I trudged along the dusty road, remembering the last time I'd made this journey, riding in luxury.

I couldn't stop thinking about Crispus, Tiro and Felix. They might be somewhere on the road; they might be imprisoned again. There was no way of knowing.

And the women at the villa – they must be very anxious by now. We had set out for a short visit to Rome, and not come back for days. Maybe Crispus and

Felix would never come back... What was I going to tell them?

At a wayside fountain, I stopped for a drink and a rest. I sat down wearily in the shade of a tree. Then I must have gone to sleep, for the next thing I knew was a voice speaking my name.

"Come on, wake up, Bryn. Unless you want to walk the rest of the way?"

That sounded like Crispus...

I sat up and rubbed my eyes. It was Crispus. There was a carriage by the fountain; Tiro was giving the horses a drink. Felix waved to me from the back seat. Oh, it was good to see them!

"So you got away all right?" I said, like an idiot.

"Yes. Thanks to you, Bryn."

Felix moved his injured foot off the carriage seat to make room for me. I got in thankfully, and only then noticed that Septimus was there too. But even the presence of Septimus could not dampen my spirits.

As we set off again, the others told me how they'd managed to escape. When Felix could not stagger any further, a complete stranger took pity on them. He let them hide in his home until morning.

"We don't even know his name," said Crispus. "He wouldn't tell us."

Septimus had helped them too. He'd let them borrow his carriage for the journey to the villa. Then he'd decided to go with them, for he wanted to see Domitia.

I noticed he was unusually quiet during the journey. He didn't try to take over the conversation; he seemed to be deep in thought. But I didn't pay him much attention.

"I wonder how many of our friends got away," I said.

"Cassius didn't," said Crispus. "We saw him at the far end of a street, surrounded by soldiers. And Micah never got out at all. As for the others, I just don't know..."

"Maybe we'll never know," said Felix.

We began to talk about the future. Obviously it would be foolish to return to Rome. Even the villa might not be safe. If the soldiers couldn't find any more Christians in the city, they might cast their net wider.

"We could travel south to Campania or north into Gaul," said Crispus. "In many towns there are groups of believers who would help us. Or we could go even further afield, to a place where no one has heard the good news of Jesus."

Tiro looked round from the driving seat. He said, "The Emperor's a fool. By driving all the Christians out of Rome, he's actually helping to spread the gospel."

I tried to look warningly at him. Was it safe to talk like this in front of Septimus?

"It's all right," Crispus said to me. "You can speak quite freely. All of us here belong to God's kingdom."

"Yes," said Felix, "even Septimus. Don't look so shocked, Bryn!"

I couldn't help it. I found myself staring at Septimus. Of course, I knew that all sorts of people could become Christians. God would never turn away anyone who came to him, even murderers and thieves. But

Septimus... He was the last person I'd ever have expected...

Fortunately he didn't notice my reaction. He was gazing into the distance. On his face was a look I'd never seen before, a look of peace. Like a man who has been on a long, hard journey, but has come safely home at last.

***

Domitia noticed a difference in him, too.

"What's happened to Septimus?" I heard her asking Crispus the following day. "He's being so kind to me. He even said sorry for the way he used to treat me! I couldn't believe it!"

Crispus tried to tell her what had caused the change. She listened doubtfully.

"I don't suppose it will last long," she said. "He'll be back to his old self in a day or two. But while it lasts I shall enjoy it."

I strolled through the garden to where Felix was sitting, his foot propped up on a bench. He had an admiring audience – his mother and the three children – as he told the story of his attack, alone and unarmed, on a Roman soldier.

"He drew his sword, but that didn't stop me. I came out of nowhere. I jumped on him – took him completely by surprise. Knocked him out totally. You should have seen it!"

I didn't interrupt his moment of glory. When he'd finished, I said, "I've been thinking about that night,

Felix, and there's something I wanted to ask you. That fire in the kitchen – have you any idea how it started?"

He started to shake his head. Then he gave me a guilty look. "Well, actually, I... er... might have had something to do with it."

"Ha! I thought so. It was just too convenient. Felix needs something to distract the guards. Oh, look – the kitchen's on fire."

"I know it was stupid," he said. "I just didn't think. I happened to walk past the kitchen door, and I saw the fire burning, and a big jar of oil standing in the corner... I didn't think it would get out of hand the way it did."

I could see by the look on his mother's face that Felix would never hear the last of this.

"It's taught me to think twice, try not to be so reckless..." Felix paused and then grinned. "But it worked, didn't it? So what are you complaining about?"

***

That evening, needing space to think, I walked up the hill behind the house. There was an amazing sunset; the western sky was a lake of fire. Shadows were lengthening in the valley below, where a road led south towards Rome and north towards... where?

I had only the vaguest idea of what lay northwards. Italy...Gaul... mountains, rivers and sea... and then Britain, my homeland, far away on the edge of the empire.

That sudden homesickness stabbed at my heart again. Perhaps I could go back to Britain, now that Tiro had gained his freedom. I could try to find my family, if any of them were still alive.

But would I feel at home there? Would I fit in? I had changed so much. I didn't belong in Rome, but I might not belong in Britain, either. Wherever I went on earth, I might always be homesick.

Then I looked up at the sky, glowing gold and fiery red, far brighter than the flames of burning Rome. And I remembered that golden city where pain and sorrow, loss and loneliness would vanish for ever.

That was my true home. It didn't matter where I went – I would go where God led me. The journey might be long or short. But every passing day would bring me a step closer to home.

The Edge of the Empire

Having survived a disastrous battle, slavery, and the great fire of Rome, Bryn is ready to return to one of the most dangerous and uncivilised countries in the Empire: Britain!

Although he has begun to love his life in Rome, Bryn is still a Briton at heart. He wants to know what happened after the great battle and if Conan, his brother, ever made it home.

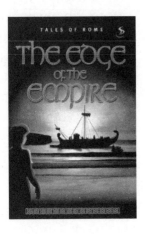

Taking his friends with him, Bryn discovers that his homeland is not as he left it. And a new threat is looming: a second rebellion is being planned. Will it bring ruin to the people?

(Published March 2006)

ISBN 1 84427 167 6

You can buy this book at your local Christian bookshop, or online at www.scriptureunion.org.uk/publishing or call Mail Order direct: 08450 706 006